A LONG TIME DEAD

A LONG TIME DEAD

A MIKE HAMMER CASEBOOK

MICKEY SPILLANE and MAX ALLAN COLLINS

MYSTERIOUSPRESS.COM

OPEN ROAD

INTEGRATED MEDIA

NEW YORK

"The Big Switch" first appeared in *The Strand*, 2008.
"A Long Time Dead" first appeared in *The Strand*, 2010.
"So Long, Chief" first appeared in *The Strand*, 2013.
"Fallout" first appeared in *The Strand*, 2015.
"Dangerous Cat" first appeared in *The Strand*, 2016.
"Grave Matter" first appeared in *Crimes by Moonlight*, ed. Charlaine Harris, 2010.
"It's in the Book" first appeared in *Mysterious Bookshop Bibliomysteries*, 2014.
"Skin" first appeared in *Dutton Guilt-Edged Mystery*, 2012.

Cover art by Andy Ross

978-1-5040-3609-2

Published in 2016 by MysteriousPress.com/Open Road Integrated Media, Inc.
180 Maiden Lane
New York, NY 10038
www.mysteriouspress.com
www.openroadmedia.com

For Michaela Hamilton
the other Mike

CONTENTS

INTRODUCTION:
THE LONG AND SHORT OF IT

That this is the first Mike Hammer short story collection—and possibly the last—may surprise some casual readers. The more knowledgeable mystery fans among you will be aware that Mickey Spillane did not write many short stories about his famous private eye—arguably, not any.

The only Hammer short stories published in Mickey's lifetime were "The Night I Died" and "The Duke Alexander." The first appeared in the anthology *Private Eyes* (Signet, 1998), co-edited by Mickey and myself, and was my uncredited adaptation of an unproduced radio script from the 1950s.

The second was essentially a comical screen treatment written for Mickey Rooney (a fairly unlikely Mike Hammer!), and a modern, tongue-in-cheek retelling of one of the taller Mickey's favorite novels, *The Prisoner of Zenda* by Anthony Hope. Mickey was a big fan of such swashbucklers, citing *The Three Musketeers* by Alexandre Dumas as his favorite—not surprisingly, since the tough ending of a lovely femme fatale's execution prefigures *I, the Jury* by a century or so.

Both stories are collected in *Byline: Mickey Spillane* (Crippen & Landru, 2004), co-edited by my friend Lynn Myers and me, with Mickey's blessing. Also in that collection—which primarily gathers non-fiction Spillane material—are two faux Hammer short stories: in-house condensations by *Playboy* of his last two Hammer novels, *The Killing Man* (1989) and *Black Alley* (1997).

The absence of Mike Hammer short stories in Spillane's body of work may seem puzzling, particularly in view not only of the character's popularity but the writer's enthusiasm for shorter-form fiction. Mickey told me on several occasions that he preferred writing novelettes to novels, considering 20,000 words the ideal length for his kind of story. He grew up an enthusiast of short stories in *Black Mask* and other detective/crime pulps, and was a big fan of Carroll John Daly's short fiction about proto-Hammer Race Williams. Of Dashiell Hammett's detectives, Spillane preferred the Continental Op to Sam Spade and Nick Charles, having read the Op stories in *Black Mask* and elsewhere. Not surprisingly, the rough, tough *Red Harvest* (which had been serialized in *Black Mask*) was Spillane's favorite among Hammett's novels.

It's well-known that Spillane was a comic book scripter prior to becoming the Twentieth Century's bestselling American mystery writer. Not so well-known is that Spillane alternated scripting comics with writing filler short stories that were a necessity for comic books to meet certain postal regulations. The earliest known prose examples of Spillane's work are the pre–WWII one-page short shorts that he did for Timely, which of course became Marvel. (Among the famous characters Mickey scripted there were Captain America and Sub-Mariner.)

In the long wait between Hammer novels—*Kiss Me, Deadly* (1952) and *The Girl Hunters* (1962)—Spillane bided his time, writing short stories for *Black Mask*'s successor, *Manhunt*, and novelettes for men's adventure magazines, such as *Cavalier*, *Male*, and *Saga*. In the mid-'60s, when he began writing novels again, Spillane continued doing occasional novelettes for the men's adventure market. Works by such a hugely bestselling author (a term he disliked, preferring to be called a writer) for such relatively low-end venues may seem unlikely, but these periodicals were helmed by Mickey's pre-war comic-book editors and publishers. Loyalty ran deep with Mickey.

My friendship with Mickey lasted over several decades, growing from my adolescent fan letters to a joint Bouchercon appearance (in Milwaukee in 1981), and eventually to collaborations on mystery anthologies, comic books, and several films (Mickey was also my son Nathan's godfather). Getting to know a hero is a dangerous thing, but Mickey was never a disappointment to me. Though he had toughness in him, he was a gentle, generous, even sweet man—as Stacy Keach has said, "A pussycat."

Shortly before his passing in 2006, Mickey called me and said he was concerned that he would not be able to finish the Mike Hammer novel he was working on, *The Goliath Bone*. He asked if I would finish it for him, if that became necessary. I of course said that I would, and was honored to be asked. A few days later, Mickey told his wife Jane to round up everything from his three offices around their South Carolina home, and "give it all to Max—he'll know what to do."

That of course was an even greater honor. Mickey had predicted a "treasure hunt," and Jane and my wife Barb and I gathered manuscript after manuscript from those offices. The amount of unpublished material in Mickey's files was and is staggering. After we'd gathered everything, Jane, Barb and I sat around the big dining room table at the Spillane home with tall stacks of pages in front of us, a literary feast. We would go through our individual piles and occasionally someone would cry out, *"Here's a Hammer!"* Anything Mickey wrote about Hammer was the gold of this treasure hunt.

We found six Hammer novels in progress, dating back to 1947 and up to a few years before Mickey's death, and a number of shorter but significant manuscripts from which Hammer novels could be developed. In addition, there were three film scripts—one of which is now the western novel, *The Legend of Caleb York* (2015, Kensington)—and two non-Hammer novels, *Dead Street* (2007, Hard Case Crime) and *The Consummata* (2011, Hard Case Crime).

Why did Mickey leave so many unpublished, unfinished manuscripts behind? There's no one answer to that. For one thing, Mickey was an enthusiastic writer who would put something aside if he got another, potentially better idea. He was working on *King of the Weeds* (which I finished for 2014 publication) when the Twin Towers came down in 2001. Almost immediately he set *King of the Weeds* aside and turned to the NYC terrorist plot of *The Goliath Bone*.

Many of the Hammer manuscripts appear to have been set aside because of Mickey's concern that his church, the conservative Jehovah's Witnesses, would object to their content. In that regard, some of the manuscripts end right after a steamy sex scene. *The Big Bang* (completed by me for 2010 publication) appears to have been set aside when he missed a deadline and substituted an early, unpublished Hammer novel (*The Twisted Thing*, 1966 but written around 1947) . . . and he never returned to *The Big Bang*, though he often spoke of its shocking ending as a particular favorite.

In addition, Mickey was famous for defining inspiration

as "the urgent need for money." This tongue-in-cheek quip had some truth in it—during the eighteen-year period he was pulling down big bucks appearing in self-spoofing Miller Lite commercials, he wrote very little. But when Hurricane Hugo destroyed his home in 1989, he quickly wrote *The Killing Man*, the first Mike Hammer novel in almost twenty years.

In addition to the manuscripts that were well under way, we treasure hunters found a number of shorter Hammer manuscripts. These, from the very start, struck me as possible Hammer short stories. Mickey had a real way of setting a story up clearly in just a chapter or even a few pages. Knowing his work as I do, I felt confident I could take these stories in either the same direction he would have or one that he'd have approved.

This book collects the short stories I've developed from these shorter unfinished Hammer manuscripts. They have been published for the most part by Andrew Gulli in the *Strand Magazine*, starting in 2008—thank you, Andrew! The publisher of this book, Otto Penzler's Mysterious Bookshop, published my favorite of these stories, "It's in the Book," in their series of individually published bibliomystery stories. Dutton, where Mike Hammer began with *I, the Jury*, published the novelette *Skin* as an ebook (this collection marks the story's first print publication).

Several of these stories have been honored. In 2014, "So Long Chief" was Edgar-nominated and won both the PWA Shamus and the IAMTW Scribe. "The Big Switch" was selected for the *Best Crime and Mystery Stories of 2009* anthology, and "A Long Time Dead" was nominated for the CWA Dagger, a Thriller Award, and the Shamus, and was selected for Otto Penzler's anthology, *Best American Mystery Stories* of 2011. "Fallout" won the Scribe in 2016.

INTRODUCTION

With one exception, I have arranged these stories in chronological order. My approach in completing these short stories—and the novels—is to try to determine when Mickey began them and stay true to that. Hammer is a character who grows and shifts as the years pass, and the same is true of his creator. In addition to style and character aspects, there is always internal evidence—if Mike and Velda dine at the Blue Ribbon Restaurant, it's pre-1976 (the restaurant defunct by that time), especially if Hammer is drinking Pabst not Miller Lite, since that's the year those famous commercials began.

The first three stories here—"The Big Switch," "Fallout," and "A Long Time Dead"—take place in the 1960s. "So Long, Chief" and "Dangerous Cat" are 1970s stories. "It's in the Book" is a 1980s-era piece, and "Skin" is a tale set in the late 1990s. These obviously span much of the length of Mike Hammer's career.

"Grave Matter" takes place in the early 1950s, filling that in further; but I did not want to lead with that story as it's the only one here I wrote largely by myself.

In 1994, Mickey Spillane and I created a science-fiction variation on his "Mike Danger" for comic books. Mickey developed the character just before World War Two, and attempted to market it after the war, without success. In 1947, he decided to change "Danger" to "Hammer" and *I, the Jury* was the result.

Meanwhile, back in the future (the '90s), the comic book company (Big Entertainment) asked Mickey and me to develop a prose short story, which they never got around to using. Mickey had approved this story and gave me notes, but the writing was mine. In 2010, when Charlaine Harris invited me to do a horror-tinged mystery story for the MWA anthology,

Crimes by Moonlight, "Grave Matter" came to mind. I changed "Danger" back to "Hammer," and it was published under the joint Spillane/Collins byline.

So I present that particularly pulpy yarn as a change of pace, between the '60s and '70s tales, and as a glimpse at the first prose Hammer story I ever undertook.

Because these are stories from material Mickey did not complete, they occasionally foreshadow novels where the writer followed up on the same basic idea. Both "Fallout" and "Dangerous Cat" prefigure the Hammer novel, *Murder Never Knocks* (2016), in the setup of multiple attacks on the private eye's life. The two stories also, of course, resemble each other in that fashion, though they and the novel are distinctly different. "A Long Time Dead" similarly prefigures *The Killing Man* and yet is a story wholly apart.

I still plan to do a number of non-Hammer short stories, from materials in Mickey's files, and there's a possibility some of the non-Hammer fragments may lend themselves to more Mike. But this volume represents every Hammer short story developed from the shorter unfinished Spillane manuscripts that feature his famous character.

My thanks to MysteriousPress.com and Otto Penzler, who has been a key player in keeping the Spillane flame burning, starting with publishing the first three posthumous Hammer novels as well as the short story, "It's in the Book," and the collection you're about to read.

Max Allan Collins
December 2015

THE BIG SWITCH

They were going to kill Dopey Dilldocks at midnight the day after tomorrow.

He had shot and wiped out a local narcotics pusher because the guy had passed Dopey a packet of heroin that had been stepped on so many times, it wouldn't take the pain out of a pinprick. The pusher deserved it. Society said Dopey Dilldocks deserved it, too. The jury agreed and the judge laid on the death sentence. All the usual delays had been exhausted, and the law-and-order governor sure as hell wouldn't reprieve a lowlife druggie like Dopey, so the little schmoe's time to fly out of this earthly coop was now.

Nobody was ever going to notice his passing. He was just another jailhouse number—five feet seven inches tall with seven digits stamped on his shirt. On the records his name was Donald Dilbert, but along the path laid out by snorting lines of the happy white stuff, it had gotten shortened and twisted into Dopey Dilldocks.

A week ago his lawyer, a court-assigned one, had written me to say that Mister Dilbert had requested that I be a witness to his execution. And it seemed Dopey also wondered if I might stop in, ASAP, and have a final chat with him before the big switch got thrown.

In the inner office of my P.I. agency in downtown Manhattan, I handed the letter to Velda, my secretary and right-hand man, if a doll with all that raven hair and a mountain road's worth of curves could be so described. I was sitting there playing with the envelope absently while she read its contents. When she was done, she frowned and passed the sheet back to me. "Donald Dilbert . . . You mean that funny little guy who—"

"The same," I said. "The one they called Mr. Nobody, and worse."

She frowned in mild confusion. "Mike—he was only a messenger boy. He didn't even work for anybody important, did he?"

"Probably the biggest was Billy Whistler, that photographer over on Sixth Avenue. Hell, I got Dopey that job because the little guy didn't mind running errands at night."

"You know what he did over there?"

"Sure. Took proofs of the late-night photo shoots over to the magazine office."

Velda gave me an inquisitive glance.

I shook my head. "No dirty Gertie stuff—Whistler deals with advertising agencies handling big-ticket household items—freezers, stoves, air conditioners, that sort of thing. Not Paparazzi crap."

"Big agencies—so little Dopey was getting large pay?"

"Hardly. You said it yourself. He's been around for decades and started a messenger boy and that's how he wound up."

She arched an eyebrow. "Not really, Mike."

"Huh?"

"He wound up a killer. He'll wind up sitting down at midnight."

"Yeah," I nodded. "And not getting up."

She was frowning again. "Messenger boy isn't exactly big bucks, Mike. How could he afford a narcotics habit?"

"They say if you're hooked," I said, "you'll find a way."

"Maybe by dealing yourself?"

"Naw. Dopey doesn't have the brains for it."

"What kind of pusher would give a guy like that credit?"

"Nobody I know," I admitted. "Something stinks about this."

"Coming off in waves. You going to the execution? You thinking of paying him a visit first?" Her voice had a strange tone to it.

My eyes drifted up from the envelope I was fidgeting with and met hers. We both stared and neither of us blinked. I started to say something and stopped. I reached out and took the letter from her fingertips and it read it again.

Very simple legalese. The lawyer was simply passing along a request. It was only a job to him. The state would reimburse him for his professional time, which couldn't have been very much.

Before I could say anything, Velda told me, "You haven't done a freebie in a long time."

"Kitten . . ."

"You could make it a tax deduction, Mike."

"Going to an execution?"

"Giving this thing a quick look. Just a couple of days to you, but to Dopey Dilldocks, it's the rest of his life."

I shook my head. "I don't need a deduction. What's gotten into you? The poor slob has been through a trial, he was declared guilty of first-degree murder and now he's paying the penalty."

Very quietly Velda asked, "How do you know it really *was* first-degree?"

3

I shook my head again, this time in exasperation. "There was a squib in the paper."

"No," she said insistently. "Dopey didn't even rate a 'squib.' There was an article on narcotics and what strata of society uses them. It gave a range from high-priced movie stars to little nothings like Donald Dilbert, who'd just been found guilty in his murder trial."

"Wasn't a big article," I said lamely.

"No. And Dopey was just a footnote. Still . . . you recognized his name, didn't you?"

I nodded.

"And what did you think?"

"That Dopey had finally come up in the world."

"Baloney. You were thinking, how the hell could Dopey Dilldocks plan and execute a first-degree murder—weren't you?"

She had me and she knew it. For the few times I had used the schlub to run messages, I had gotten to know him just enough to recognize his limitations. He knew the red light that meant stop was on the top and he wouldn't cross the street until the bottom one turned green, and that type of mentality didn't lay out a first-degree kill.

"So?" she asked.

The semblance of a grin was starting to twitch at her lips and she took a deep breath. The way she was built, deep breathing should have had a law against it.

I said, "Just tell me something, doll. You barely know Dopey. You haven't got the first idea of what this is all about. How come you're on his side suddenly?"

"Because I'd give him a couple of bucks to buy me a sandwich for lunch and he'd always bring the change back in the bag. He never stole a cent from me."

"What a recommendation," I said sourly.

"The best," she came back at me. "Besides, we need to get out of this office for a while. It's a beautiful Spring day, the bills are paid, there's money in the bank, nothing's on the platter at the moment and—"

"And we might pass one of those 'Medical Examination, Wedding Ceremony, One Day' places, right?"

"Could be," she said. "Anyway, we could use a day trip."

"A day trip where?"

"Someplace quiet upstate."

"A little hotel on the river, you mean?"

"That's right."

Sing Sing.

A looker like Velda could have caused a riot in places that didn't consist of concrete and cells, and anyway the court-appointed lawyer could only arrange for one visitor. So she sat in the car in a lot outside the massive stone facility, while I sat in a gray-brick room in one of several cubicles with phones and wire-reinforced glass.

Dopey was a forty-something character who might have been sixty. He had a gray pallor that had been his before he entered the big house, and his runny nose and rheumy eyes spoke of the weed and coke he'd consumed for decades. Smack was never his scene, as his fairly plump frame indicated. His hair, once blond and thick, was white and wispy now, and his face was a chinless, puffy thing.

"I think they musta framed me, Mike," he said. He had a mid-range voice with a hurt tone like a teenage boy who just got the car keys taken away.

My hat was on the little counter. I spoke into the phone,

looking at his pitiful puss. "And you want me to pry it off of you, Dopey? You might have given me more notice."

"I know. I know." Phone to his ear, shaking his head, he had the demeanor of a guy in a confessional. Too bad I wasn't in the sin-forgiving game.

"So why now, Dopey?"

"I just been thinking, Mike. I been going back through my whole life. They say it flashes through your brain, right before you die? But I been going through my life, one crummy photo at a time."

I sat forward. "Is that a figure of speech, Dopey? Or are you getting at something?"

Dopey swallowed thickly. "I never gave nobody no trouble, Mike. I never did crime, not even for my habit. I worked hard. Double shifts. Never made no enemies. I'm a nobody like they used to call me, just a damn inanity."

He meant nonentity, but I let it go.

"So you been thinking," I said. "What have you been thinking?"

"I think it all goes back to me sending that photo to LaSalle."

"LaSalle? You don't mean *Governor* LaSalle?"

The chinless head bobbed. "About six months ago, I ran across this undeveloped roll of film. It was in a yellow envelope marked Phi U 'April Fool's Party.'"

Where the hell was this going?

"I remembered that night. Up at Solby College? It was wild. Lots of kids partying—girls with their tops off. Crazy."

"When was this?"

"Twenty years ago—April first, like I said. I was taking pictures all over the frat house. They was staging stuff—lots of fake murders and suicides and crazy stuff right out of a horror movie."

"And you got shots of some of that?"

Dopey's head bobbed again. "I was going around campus taking oddball pictures. I even got some 'peeper' type shots through a sorority house window, where this girl was undressing—then this guy pretends to strangle her. It was very real looking. Frankly, it scared me silly, it was so real looking."

"Is that why you didn't develop the film?"

"No, the frat guys never paid me, so I said screw it. But when I ran across that roll of film, I don't know why, I just remembered how pretty that girl was—the one that played at getting strangled? She had her top off and . . . well, I can develop my own pics, you know."

"And you did?"

"I did, Mike. And the guy doing the pretend strangling? He looked just like a young version of Governor LaSalle! So I sent it to him."

I thought my eyes would pop out of my skull. "You *what*?"

"Just as a joke. I thought he might get a kick out of it, the resemblance."

I squinted at the goofy little guy. "Be straight with me, Dopey—you didn't try to blackmail him with that, did you?"

"No! I didn't think it was *really* him—just looked like him."

My stomach was tight. "What if it really was him, Dopey? And what if that wasn't an April Fool's stunt you snapped?"

Dopey swallowed again and nodded. "That was what started me thinking, Mike. That's why I hoped you might come see me."

"You told your lawyer about this?"

"No! How do I know I could trust him? He works for the state, too, don't he?"

But he trusted me. This pathetic little doper trusted me to get him out of a jam only an idiot could get into.

Well, maybe I was an idiot, too. Because I told him I'd look into it, and to keep his trap shut till he heard from me next.

"When will that be, Mike?"

"It won't be next week," I said, and got my hat and went.

Our jaunt upstate didn't last long. I called Captain Pat Chambers of Homicide from the road and he was waiting at our favorite little deli restaurant, down the block from the Hackard Building. Pat was in a back booth working on a soft drink and some fries. We slid in opposite him.

The NYPD's most decorated officer wore a lightweight gray suit that went with the gray eyes that had seen way too much—probably too much of me, if you asked him.

"Okay," he said, with no hellos, just a nod to Velda, "what are you getting me into now?"

"Nothing. You found something?"

Those weary eyes slitted, and this time his nod was for me. "Twenty years ago, April second, a coed from Solby College was found strangled, dumped on a country road."

"And nobody got tagged for it?"

"No. There were some stranglings on college campuses back then—mostly in the Midwest—and this one got lumped in as one of the likely unsolved murders that went along with the rest."

"Didn't they catch that guy?"

"Yeah. He rode Old Sparky in Nebraska. But the Solby College murder, he never copped to."

"Interesting."

"Is it?" Pat sat forward. "Mike, do I have to tell you there's no statute of limitations on murder? That no murder case is truly ever closed till somebody falls? If you *have* something . . ."

"I do have something."

"What, man?"

"A hunch."

The gray eyes closed. He loved me like a brother, but he could hate me the same way. "Mike . . . do I have to give you the speech again?"

"No. I got it memorized. Tell me about Governor LaSalle."

The eyes snapped open. Pat looked at Velda for help and didn't get any. "You start with a twenty year-old murder, chum, and then you ask about . . . What do you *mean*, tell me about Governor LaSalle?"

"He got elected as a law-and-order guy. How's he doing?"

Pat waved that off. "I stay out of politics."

"Which is why you been on the force since Jesus was a baby and still aren't an inspector. What's the skinny on the Gov?"

His voice grew hushed. "You've heard the stories."

"Have I?"

"I can't say anything more."

"Then you can't confirm that an Internal Affairs investigation into the Governor's relationship with a high-end prostitution ring got shut down because of political pressure?"

"No."

"Can you deny it?"

"No."

"What *can* you tell me, buddy?"

He stared at the soft drink like he was trying to will it into a beer. Then, very quietly, he said, "The word is, our esteemed governor is a sex addict. He uses State Patrol Officers as pimps. It's a lousy stinking disgrace, Mike, but it's not my bailiwick. Or yours."

"What about the rumors that he has a little sex shack

upstate? A little cabin in the mountains where he meets with female constituents?"

Pat's grin was pretty sick. "That's impossible, Mike. Our governor's a happily married man."

Then Pat stopped a waitress and asked for a napkin. She gave him one, and Pat scribbled something on it, something fairly detailed. Then he folded the napkin, gave it to me, and slipped out of the booth.

"Get the check, Mike," he said, and was gone.

Velda frowned over at me curiously. "What is it?"

"Directions."

This time I took the drive upstate alone, much to Velda's displeasure. But she knew not to argue, when I said I had something to do that I didn't want her part of.

The shade-topped drive dead-ended at a gate, but I pulled over into the woods half a mile before I got there. I was in a black t-shirt and black jeans with the .45 on my hip, not in its usual shoulder sling. The night was cool, the moon was full and high, and ivory touched the leaves with a picture-book beauty. An idyllic Spring night, if you weren't sitting on Death Row waiting for your last tomorrow.

It was a cabin, all right, logs and all, but probably bigger than what Old Abe grew up in—a single floor with maybe four or five rooms. Out front a lanky state trooper was having a smoke. Maybe I was reading in, but he seemed disgusted, whether with himself or his lot in life, who knows?

I spent half an hour making sure that trooper was alone. It seemed possible another trooper or two might be walking the perimeter, but security was limited to that one bored trooper. And that cruiser of his was the only vehicle. I had expected the Governor to have his own wheels, but I'd been wrong.

Positioned behind a nice big rock with trees at my back, I watched for maybe fifteen minutes—close enough that no binoculars were needed—before the Governor himself, in a purple smoking jacket and silk pajamas right out of Hefner's closet, exited with a petite young woman on his arm. He was tall and white-haired and handsome in a country club way. She was blonde and very curvy, in a blue halter top and matching hot pants. If she was eighteen, I was thirty.

At first I thought she had on a lot of garish make-up, then I got a better look and realized she had a bloody mouth and one of her eyes was puffy and black.

The bastard had been beating her!

She was carrying not a purse but a wallet—clutched in one hand like the lifeline it was, a pro doing business with rough trade like the Gov—and her gracious host gave her a little peck on the cheek. Then he took her by the arm and passed her to the trooper like a beer they were sharing.

I could hear most of what LaSalle said to his trooper/pimp. "Take Miss So-and-So home, and come pick me up. I want to be back to the mansion by midnight."

The trooper nodded dutifully, opened the rear of the cruiser like the prostie was a suspect not a colleague, and then they were off in a crunch of gravel and puff of dust.

There was a back door and opening it with burglar picks took all of twenty seconds. The Gov wasn't much on security. I came in through a small kitchen, where you could hear a shower on in a nearby bathroom.

That gave me the luxury of getting the lay of the land, but there wasn't much to see. The front room had a fireplace with a mounted fish over it and a couch and an area to watch TV and a little dining area. I spent most of my time poking around in his office, which had a desk and a few file cabinets, and a comfortable wood-and-cushions chair off by a window. That's where I was sitting, .45 in hand, when he came in only in his boxer shorts, toweling his white hair.

He looked pudgy and vaguely dissipated, and he didn't see me at first.

In fact, I had to chime in with, "Good evening, Governor. Got a moment for a taxpayer?"

He dropped the towel like it had turned to flame. He wheeled toward me, his ice-blue eyes wide, though his brow was furrowed.

"What the hell . . . *who* the hell . . . ?"

"I'm Mike Hammer," I said. "Maybe you heard of me."

Now he recognized me.

"Good God, man," he said. "What are you doing here?"

"I was in the neighborhood. Go ahead. Sit at your desk. Make yourself comfortable. We need to talk."

His shower must have been hot, because his doughy flesh had a red cast. But the red in his face had nothing to do with needles of water.

"There's a trooper on his way back here right now," the Governor said.

"Yeah, but he has to drop your date off first. Tell me, was that shiner and bloody mouth all of it? Or would I find whip marks under that halter top?"

He had gone from startled to indignant in about a second. Now he made a similar trip from indignant to scared. I waved the gun, and he padded over to the desk and got settled in his leather chair.

"What is this," he said, "a shakedown?"

"You mean, lowlife P.I. stakes out sex-addict governor and tries for a quick kill? Maybe. Your family has money. Your wife's family has more."

He sighed. The ice-blue eyes were more ice than blue. "You have a reputation as a hardass, Hammer. But I don't see you as a blackmailer. Who hired you? One of these little chippies? Some little tramp get a little more than she bargained for? Then she should've picked another trade."

"You know, they been talking about you running for president. You really think you can keep a lid on garbage like this?"

He gestured vaguely. "I can reach in my desk drawer and get a check book, and write you out a nice settlement for your client, and another for you, and we'll forget this happened. I just want your guarantee there will be no . . . future payments."

I shifted a little. The .45 was more casual in my hand now. "I have a client, all right, Gov. His name is Dopey Dilldocks."

He frowned. "Your *client* is a murderer."

"No, Gov. You are. My client is an imbecile who thought you might be amused by what he thought was a gag photo taken years ago, involving either you or more likely some college kid with a resemblance to you. But that was no gag—you really strangled that girl. You hadn't quite got a grip, let's say, on your habit, your sick little sex hobby."

The big bare-chested white-haired man leaned forward. "Hammer, that's nonsense. If this is true, where *are* these supposed photos?"

"Oh, hell. Your boys cleaned up on that front right after you framed Dopey. You've got underworld connections, like so many law-and-order frauds. You can't maintain a sadistic habit like yours without high friends in low places—you're tied in with the call girl racket on its uppermost levels, right?"

"You don't know what you're talking about, Hammer."

I stood. I was smiling. I wouldn't have wanted to be on the other end of that smile, but it was a smile.

"Look, Gov—I'm not after blackmail money. All I want is a phone call from the governor."

He frowned up at me. "What?"

"You've seen the old movies." I pointed at the fat phone on his desk. "You're going to call the warden over at Sing Sing, and you are going to tell him that you have reason to believe Donald Dilbert aka Dilldocks is innocent, and you are issuing the prisoner a full pardon."

"Isn't not that easy, Hammer . . ."

"It's just that easy. Then you're calling the Attorney General and informing her that you've made that call, and that the pardon is official."

And that's what he did. Under the barrel of my .45, but he did it. And he was a good actor, like so many politicians. He didn't tip it—sounded sincere as hell.

When he'd hung up after his conversation with the Attorney General, he said, "What now?"

I came around behind the desk and stood next to the seated LaSalle. "Now you get a piece of paper out of your desk drawer. I want this in writing."

His face seemed to relax. "All right, Hammer. If I pardon Dilldocks, this ends here?"

"It will end here."

He nodded, the ice-blues hooded, his silver hair catching moonlight through the window behind him. He reached in his bottom-right hand drawer and came back with the .22 revolver and he fired it right at me.

The click on the empty cylinder made him blink.

Then my .45 was in his face. "I took the liberty of removing that cartridge when I had a look around in here. Lot of fire-arms accidents at home, you know."

My left hand came around, gripped his right hand clutching the .22, and swung the barrel around until he was looking cross-eyed at it.

"But there's another slug waiting, Gov," I said, "should the need arise."

And my hand over his hand, my finger over his finger, squeezed the trigger. A bullet went in through his open mouth and the inside of his head splattered the window behind him, blotting out the moon.

"Some sons of bitches," I said to the suicide, "just don't deserve a reprieve."

FALLOUT

Something felt wrong.

It wasn't the little gusts of wind that had rain smell in them, or that strange quiet that comes at night in New York when nobody expects it. Sometimes it's evening and the cabbies park for a coffee break, and other times it's into the wee-hours morning when there isn't even a fire siren going anywhere in the city. All you can feel is that nobody's moving and you wonder why. There really should be a horn honking somewhere or a scream someplace.

But there's nothing at all.

You look down the street and you're alone. It's Lexington Avenue and Thirty-ninth and nothing's happening. Helen Fainey was a hooker who worked that corner until a drunk driver wiped her out, but so far nobody else has taken her place. A truck growls by and the guy behind the wheel drops a cigarette out the window with a twitchy little motion like he senses something wrong, too.

The traffic light goes red and I stop at the curb. No cars coming either way and I could go right across, but I don't. Like the late Fainey dame, I almost got tagged by some speeding soused-up asshole when I crossed here last night.

The light turns green but I don't cross. Empty street or not.

Quietly, I pull my trenchcoat collar up and my hat brim down, and say, "Damn."

Half a block to my right an all-night diner's sign is blinking and I cut toward it. I'd never been there before but the counterman gives me that look that makes me as a regular city slob and starts pouring me a coffee before I even ask for it. I order a hard buttered roll, dunk it and it tastes swell.

Then what was wrong?

The counterman said, "Lousy night, eh, mac? Cold's comin'. More damn rain."

"Could be worse," I told him in a way that said the roll was great but hold the side order of talk. He was fine with that. He rubbed the counter with his dirty wet rag.

Then I knew *what was wrong.*

For about two months now, I would hit the rack around midnight, then wake up at three and there was nothing left but to walk it off. And it came to me I had been tracking down the same path the same way at the same time for all that while. This was the first time since the Salem shooting that I'd even crossed a street to a different place.

Stupidly, I had set a pattern. Now I knew what that asshole driver was aiming at the other night. Make that *who*. Only he wasn't drunk and he wasn't an asshole, either. He was a pro, a very specialized one.

And that fight some hothead started at the Forty-second Street BMT subway station last week wasn't just some idiocy that almost took three spectators and me onto the tracks.

And that long-haired buck-tooth druggie trying to mug me on Eighth Avenue wasn't a simple stick-up try, it was a for fucking real hit that didn't quite go down. Not after I broke the jerk's arm, jammed his shiv in his ass and kicked his guts loose for trying that action on somebody sober and big enough to walk that area alone.

But I'd been stupid then, too.

That was no mugging. That prick had been trying to kill me. He'd come in with a grin and a knife held low in his palm with the cutting edge up and the swipe he took was pure professional. Anybody else he would have taken out, but I'd been tuned into garbage like that for a long time and put him down like I was swatting a bug.

A long time.

Time.

It was catching up with me. Ten years ago, I would never have let myself get so sloppy. I had been following patterns those other times too. Back then I would have smelled it sooner. Well, I could smell it now, the dark wet clouds rolling in around me. Seconds ago, I'd been blissfully sitting here in an off-street diner dunking my buttered hard roll in hot coffee, when what I should have been doing was watch my damn ass *. . . because somebody was coming after it.*

Great feeling. Scary as hell. I don't mind somebody coming head on at me, but sneak-attack crap that you can't anticipate is something the hell else. All you know is that somebody has a kill on his mind and you are the target. And making it worse was knowing they were pros.

Pros, but on the low-end side. They'd missed three times. *But now I smelled them.*

I paid the bill, gave the counterman a buck and went back out onto the street. The dull acidity of the city was gone now. The total boredom that seeps into Manhattan natives wasn't part of me any longer. For the first time in a long time, I had that itchy feeling again and it was running up and down my back like a lover's fingers and if anybody saw me grinning, they'd wonder why my teeth were showing when really nothing was funny at all.

So I stayed with the pattern and took the rest of the walk that traced the path I had been following for months. It was getting cooler but I opened my trenchcoat and unbuttoned my suitcoat for easier access to the .45 under my left arm. Finally I got to the Hackard Building, where my office had been till the renovations got under way, and went into the lobby where old Gus presided after hours over the facelift in progress.

Only Gus wasn't there. His crumpled lunch bag was on the big crate he'd been using for a desk and the *Daily News* was under it, but he wasn't there. Then I edged along the wall and saw the bulk jammed under the crate and Gus was there after all.

You don't need doctors or coroners or medical examiners to tell you when somebody is dead. Not this kind of dead. You say, "Shit," because you *knew* this dead somebody and he was a great old guy who was your friend. And because he was your friend, *you* are the reason he is stuffed inside a wooden crate with bullet holes in him leaking red.

And there was no reason for Gus dying except that I'd broken pattern to have that buttered hard roll and coffee and somebody came looking for me and Gus got suspicious. Some killer tried to make his presence seem innocent and a lobby guy who knew what it meant to have Mike Hammer in his building had betrayed disbelief on his face and got dead for his trouble.

But somebody else would get dead now.

With .45 in hand, I prowled the lobby and any open doors off of it to see if the killer was still around. No surprise that he wasn't—he'd killed Gus out of some kind of reflex and wouldn't be hanging around to see if I ever did show up.

I folded a Kleenex around my fingers, lifted the phone on Gus's crate, and dialed. Even out of a deep sleep, the voice was alert and controlled.

Just one word. It wasn't even a question: "Yes."

Flat.

"Sorry to break a promise, kid," I said.

". . . Mike?"

"Yeah."

There wasn't any friendliness in either of our voices. It had been a long time since Pat and I had that old smooth feeling.

"I'm on one," I said.

"You always are."

If he wanted to know, he needed to ask. I let a few seconds go past.

Finally he said, "Where." No question inflection at all.

"The lobby of the Hackard Building," I told him. "Somebody murdered the lobby guy. Gus Smalley."

"Hell. That nice old guy?"

"That nice old guy. I'll wait."

"Yes you will," he said and hung up.

Pat played by all the rules. He always had. The nearest squad car came in, did their bit, the detectives followed and a forensics team showed up to make it an official crime scene. Pat was right behind them, looking like a jaded New York cop who had seen too many dead bodies, attended too many autopsies and been part of too many take-downs. And he had seen and done all that and more. But Pat Chambers jaded? Forget it.

Hell, he didn't even have to be there. He wasn't on duty. He was a Captain of Homicide and the only reason I called him was to shove a needle up his tail. Finding me at a murder scene meant he'd have to deal with me again. And maybe we could start putting that falling out behind us.

He played it cool. *Good old Pat Chambers*, I thought. *The Charlie Brown of the NYPD.* They passed him over for inspector. Some said that was because he was friends with a "controversial" private investigator. Really it was because he stuck to the rule book. Mr. Honesty. Straight shooter. Go against the politicians and be right when they are wrong and see where it gets you.

"Let's hear it, Mike," he said.

He was as big as me but not quite as heavy. He left his hat on, like me. Just two tired trenchcoats facing each other.

"Not much to tell." I shrugged. "I came in here to say hello like every night lately. And there he was."

Pat had those funny gray-blue eyes that can seem calm when really they've gone sour. "And there he was," he repeated.

I shrugged again.

"Why?"

"Beats me."

"Bullshit. What are you up to, Mike?"

"Not a damn thing. When did you get so damn nasty, Pat? I didn't think police officials used that kind of language around the general populace."

"Screw you, buddy."

He pointed a finger at me that said, *Stay put.*

Seconds dragged out into minutes while he looked around, checking the work of the plainclothes officers and the forensics team. Wasn't like Pat was somebody new. He was an old hand and he wanted to see it all for himself. And whatever he saw, he remembered.

Then he came back over and rocked on his heels gently. The eyes were hooded now. His head back.

"This is fallout from the Salem shooting," he said, "isn't it?"

"How should I know?"

"Yeah. How should *you* know."

"Come on, Pat. What's all this beefing about? I didn't kill that slob. I shot him. That's all."

For a second, fire flared in his eyes. "You just shot him?" He paused, groping for words. "Hell, Mike, you didn't just shoot him—you shot the *shit* out of him. You tore his hands up, you mangled his feet, you got his ribs broken, his teeth knocked out . . . and that was *all*?"

"How many ways do you want me to paint it?" I asked him. "I heard shots coming from that lawyer's office and then this Salem character I'd seen in the papers burst out. He was a big sweaty wild-eyed guy with a .357 magnum in his fist, running toward the stairwell. Anyway, a lot of that damage was from the fall he took."

"The first one was a hip shot," Pat stated flatly.

"There wasn't time to aim."

"And then you took his feet out from under him with the second shot."

"Right," I agreed. "Both feet. They just happened to be lined up perfectly."

"Oh, so you *did* have time to aim."

"You got it all wrong, kiddo."

"You're saying they were, what? Lucky shots?"

I shrugged. "Too bad he fell down the stairs."

"Too bad?"

"Yeah. He was screaming real nice up till then."

His eyebrows rose. "You enjoyed it?"

"Didn't bother me."

Pat shook his head and grunted. "Your luck is amazing, pal. You nail an escaped, convicted murderer, you damn near destroy the guy and you get the greatest press coverage in the world. Nobody even *inquires* what other options you had, nobody wants to know if you were aware of the police cordon around the building, or why the hell you were there to start with."

"I was there on unrelated business. Anyway, Pat, you forgot the good side of it."

"Sure. Remind me about the 'good' side."

"Thanks to me, you NYPD guys put Rennie Salem under arrest, his rights were read him and he confessed on the spot. Wasn't like his lawyer could talk him out of it, since he just shot the guy. And all I had to do was show my license and gun permit and put in a cameo appearance at the inquest."

They had Old Gus laid out now, getting him ready for the body bag. He look shrunken in his coveralls, like the bullets had let all the air out of him.

"This had nothing to do with you," Pat said.

"Not that I know of."

"But it could have."

"It's the Hackard Building. I've been dropping by at a fairly regular time. Figure it out yourself. You're a detective. Anyway, that's the rumor."

He gestured toward what used to be Gus. "Am I supposed to believe you aren't gonna go off half-cocked over this thing?"

"Fully cocked, Pat. Always fully cocked."

"Old joke. Bad joke. You can go, Mr. Hammer."

"One more thing, Captain Chambers."

"Yeah?"

"You might want to check into what Salem's brothers are up to."

An eyebrow rose. "His older two brothers are in stir. You know that."

"But the younger ones running that garage in Queens? Suspected of running a chop shop? They aren't. Wonder what they were doing tonight?"

The gray-blue eyes were lasers now. "You *do* think this is fallout from the Salem shooting."

I turned over a hand. "I think it's the kind of thing you and your little elves can track easier than me. Since you don't want me getting involved or anything."

His grunt was almost a laugh. "Anything else I can do for you?"

"Yeah. See if anybody wanted Gus out of the way. He's who got murdered, after all. You're good at that kind of thing."

His smile was mostly sneer. "Which means you don't want to screw with it, since you figure this was about you, not him."

"I'm just trying to be helpful."

"Sure you are."

I didn't bother saying goodbye.

Neither did Pat.

I was camped out on the leather couch in the outer office when Velda came in. My coat was off and my shoes and tie too, but I hadn't been sleeping.

"You here early?" she asked, hanging up her poncho in the closet. "Or late?"

I sat up, put my feet on the floor, rubbed my unshaved face with both hands. "Split the difference, kitten."

Velda walked with liquid confidence over to an antique

desk that was a happy anachronism amid modern office furnishings in the space we were renting while the Hackard Building renovation was under way. She tossed the *Daily News* there that she'd brought in under her arm.

She was tall enough not to need heels but she wore them anyway, emphasizing the kind of high-breasted, long-legged figure that could make a guy's eyes water. His mouth, too. Her raven pageboy brushed her shoulders, making tiny whispers on the cotton of the simple white blouse. She made it and that black skirt seem like something out of Frederick's of Hollywood.

She went over to start some coffee and said, "Another sleepless night?"

"Naw. I got a good three hours, anyway."

Anybody who thought Velda was strictly here for decorative value didn't know the score. She was my secretary and secret weapon . . . and partner in Michael Hammer Investigations, right down to her PI ticket and the .22 automatic in her purse.

"So," she said, getting behind her desk and glancing at page two of the *News*, "I suppose you and Gus talked sports till the sun came up again."

"The sun came up," I said. "But I didn't talk to Gus."

I told her.

Halfway through it she came over and sat next to me, putting an arm around my shoulder. "You liked that old guy, didn't you?"

"He was nobody special. Just another old fart waiting out his pension and spouting how the coaches stink these days and the fighters are just a bunch of pansies since Marciano."

"I liked him, too. You don't think he was the target, do you?"

"No. But Pat's looking into that." I shrugged. "He's good for something, anyway."

"Don't be so hard on him," she said. "You'll be friends again one of these days. . . . You figure this is payback courtesy of the Salem brothers?"

"I've got Pat looking into that, too."

She squeezed my hand. "So . . . where do we come in? Or do we?"

"Oh, we come in all right. You remember that hooker at Lex and Thirty-ninth who I saw get run down a couple weeks ago?"

She nodded. "Helen something. You gave a statement at the scene, but it didn't go anywhere. They found the car with the plates you reported, and it was stolen. Some joyriding punk off on a drunken tear."

"That's what they thought at the time. That's what *I* thought."

I told her about my own recent brush with a drunk driver, and the subway incident. I'd told her about the mugging, back when it happened. She put it together immediately.

She spoke as she fetched coffee for us. "You've been out on your insomniac walks, every night passing by where the Fainey woman got it. Somebody noticed. Somebody who thought Mike Hammer was looking into things and planning to do something about it—you do have a reputation for that."

"Yeah." I sipped the coffee. She got the cream and sugar just right. "Lots of people know about my altruistic nature."

She was sitting beside me again. "Somebody figured you were coming after them, and also figured to beat you to the punch."

I thought about it. "I didn't really get a look at the driver who nailed the Fainey dame. I was way the hell across the street."

"Somebody doesn't know that." She half-turned and her fanny made the leather couch squeak. "Did you know her?"

"Not really. She was just somebody I walked by. She came on to me first time I passed, I told her the score, and after that it was a nod or hello."

"Listen, Mike—these three tries on you . . . could it have been the same guy?"

I frowned. "Possible. The only one I got a good look at was that hippie mugger."

A half smile blossomed. "Mike, hippies aren't muggers. The peace-and-love crowd don't pack switchblades."

"If they need drug money they do."

"Did he look strung-out, this guy?"

"No," I admitted. "So it was a . . . costume? A disguise?"

She shrugged. "*Could* it have been? Could the long hair have been a wig?"

I nodded. No matter how much sleep I'd missed last night, I felt wide awake now, thanks to her. "It sure as hell could. And the blurred glimpse I got of the driver who nearly clipped me is consistent with the better look I got at that mugger."

"So . . . do we go from mugger to mug books? Why don't I call Pat and you can go down and—"

I raised a hand to stop her. "No, Vel. Let's let Pat do his cop thing. He has solid leads to follow—the Salem brothers, Gus's private life. What we have is a theory."

"But a good one, Mike."

I grinned at her. "Damn straight. I'll take your theories over facts any day, sugar."

"Thanks. So where do we start?"

I finished my coffee and went over and put the cup on the table by the percolator. Then I paced and talked as I thought.

"Kitten, we have a guy who was involved in one vehicular killing and another near-one where I'm concerned. That's a common denominator that makes me suspect the Fainey woman was a hit, not an accident."

Still seated on the couch, her knees primly together, she said, "A car as a murder weapon is a very *specialized* choice. That's a hit man with an M.O. we can track."

I kept pacing. "That's right. He only went with the subway gag and the mugging bit because I might be on the lookout for another vehicular try. But we're forgetting the main point."

She was, as usual, ahead of me. "Helen Fainey was a target. Somebody *paid* to have her run down 'accidentally.'"

"Which means the person behind the attempted hits on me isn't necessarily the hit man, but—"

"Whoever hired him," she finished.

I came to a stop in front of her. "So that's where I'll start. With the first victim, Helen Fainey. You work on tracking our driver. Call Pat—he'd do anything for you, doll. Ask him about suspected hit men who fit the bill. Check with the insurance companies we do business with to see if they have names of individuals suspected of staging accidents for payouts."

That lush red-lipsticked mouth turned wry on me. "I spend the afternoon on the phone, with a cop and some insurance men, and you go out and chat up hookers?"

I grinned at her. "Honey, why would I want hamburger when I have filet at home?"

"First of all, I don't live at your home. Second of all, you are very much a hamburger kind of guy."

"That's just plain mean, doll."

She stood and faced me. In those heels, we were damn near eye level. "Anyway, you have to postpone your inquiries till this afternoon, or late morning at least. You have an appointment at ten with a potential client."

"When did that come in?"

"Late yesterday afternoon." She brushed by me and went to her desk to check her appointment book, frowning. "Mike . . . this is odd. Very damn odd."

"What is?"

She glanced over, the frown deepening. "I don't know why I didn't remember . . . why it didn't ring a bell . . ."

"What?"

The big brown eyes showed white all around. "Your ten o'clock appointment is with a Mr. Andrew Fainey."

He sat across from me in the client's chair with Velda seated just behind him to his right, where she could take notes and make eye contact with me.

Andrew Fainey was gray. Hair, eyes, complexion, well-trimmed mustache, even the business exec's fabled gray flannel suit. Somewhere in his mid-fifties, he was trim, tall and sadder than a wet Sunday afternoon.

"I don't know where Betty and I went wrong with Helen, Mr. Hammer." His voice had color where the rest of him didn't, a mellow thing worthy of a radio announcer but without the bounce. "She was such a good girl, growing up. Then in high school she started going out with this . . . greasy duck-tail character with a hot rod. Drinking, out to all hours, disobedient, smart-mouthed, and her grades just went to hell. Not a new story, I know."

He was from Cincinnati, Ohio, where he owned "the most successful ad agency in the Tri-State area."

"Helen got pregnant in her senior year," he said. "She had the baby, wanted to keep it, but we . . . I'm afraid we pressured her into giving it up for adoption. She moved out after that. Came east. There were phone calls, usually seeking money. Occasional letters, the same. Waitressing at first. Lately she told us she was working at a boutique in the East Village. We didn't know . . . didn't know what she *really* did for a living until the police contacted us about . . . about what happened."

He was apparently past tears, but the dignified if well-grooved gray face was nothing if not morose.

I said, "What can I do for you, Mr. Fainey?"

He sat forward a little. "You were a witness, Mr. Hammer. What did you see?"

"I saw what appeared to be a drunk driver lose control and come up over the curb and run down your daughter. It was after three in the morning and I was across the street. I didn't get a look at the guy. She was gone when I got to her. That was all in the police report."

His eyebrows lifted a quarter of an inch. "I know. That's how I learned your name. My attorney, back in Cincinnati, had heard of you. Read something about you in a true-detective magazine."

That put a small smile on Velda's lips.

"Probably something exaggerated," I said. "Is there some way I can help you, Mr. Fainey?"

His eyes narrowed. "My attorney hired a private detective here in New York when it became clear finding my daughter's killer was not a police priority. The detective talked to some other . . . young women . . . in my daughter's . . . profession.

He learned that Helen had broken off with her longtime . . ." He sighed. ". . . procurer. These girls, these women, believed Helen had been killed by this . . . pimp. To make an example of her."

"What's the detective's name?"

The question seemed to surprise him. "Oh, I never dealt with him directly. Is that important? Would you like me to call my attorney and get the number of his agency?"

"That would be helpful. We could compare notes, if you're here to have me pick up where he left off."

He nodded. "That *is* why I'm here, Mr. Hammer. This information was gathered by the investigator, and shared with the police, and nothing has come of it. I happened to be in town on business . . . we have a relationship with a top Madison Avenue firm . . . and, frankly, on impulse I thought I would look you up."

"What do you have in mind?"

"Well, there's a name I *do* have." He removed his wallet from an inside suitcoat pocket and got out a slip of paper and handed it across to me.

Tony Dyne, it said. *Grissi's.*

"I believe," he said, "it's a bar."

"I know the joint," I said. "Rough area. Nasty damn spot. What, Dyne works out of there?"

Fainey nodded. "He keeps a back booth as a kind of . . . office, from mid-evening till, oh, God knows when. Or so our private detective said. If you could go down there and size this Dyne character up, and . . . interrogate him? Perhaps we could find something out."

"Perhaps."

Velda was frowning now.

FALLOUT

"Mr. Fainey," I said. "Did that true-detective article give you any ideas about me?"

"Uh ... ideas? Such as ... ?"

"Such as maybe if this guy spooks seeing me, I might wind up ridding the world of your daughter's killer?"

He swallowed thickly. "The detective we hired said he'd done all he could. The police have no interest in pursuing this further. You do sound like the sort of man who might . . . make something happen."

Velda's eyebrows went up and one half of a smile did, too.

"A grieving father," he said, looking at the floor, "has all sorts of dark fantasies where the party or parties responsible for his child's death is concerned." Now he looked at me with blank gray eyes. "Would I like some avenging angel to wipe this foul creature off the planet? Of course. But do I expect that? No."

"What *do* you expect?"

He seemed to shrug with his entire body. "My hope is that he will betray himself to you. That he may say or do something that you, with your considerable reputation, might be able to take to the police. And that they would reopen the case and take my daughter's death seriously. You do have police connections, don't you, Mr. Hammer?"

I used to.

We settled on a retainer and he paid in cash. He was staying at the New Yorker and left his room number, where I could call him. He'd be in town till the weekend.

When he'd gone, we were back in the outer office where Velda perched on the corner of her desk with plenty of leg showing in that way a woman does who knows a guy has seen it all already.

She asked, "So . . . did our client hire your detecting skills or your gun?"

"Not sure," I said. "I'm not sure *he* knows, either."

"You still planning to spend the afternoon talking to hookers over by Lexington and Thirty-ninth?"

"No. Change of program. I still want you to check with our insurance pals, but skip calling Pat. I'm going to drop by his office."

"I didn't know you were still welcome there."

"I'm not. And do I have to tell you what else to look into while I'm gone?"

She shook her head, her smile as faint as it was pretty.

"No," she said.

The baroque old building on Centre Street near Little Italy looked more like a majestic courthouse than police headquarters. But there was nothing majestic about the aging interior of the place, including Pat's third-floor office off a bustling bullpen. The door stood open and I knocked on the jamb, leaning in.

Pat had a desk as well-ordered as his mind, file folders stacked neatly, each waiting its turn. His suitcoat was on but his tie was loose, and on the yellow legal pad in front of him was the hasty but legible evidence of hours spent the way any good detective spends them.

On the phone.

"Mind if I sit down?" I asked. "Do my taxes cover that?"

He didn't smile but he did gesture to the hardwood chair as he rocked back a little in his swivel one. Green metal filing cabinets backed him up like a police phalanx.

I sat and crossed my legs. "Ever hear of a guy named Tony Dyne?"

"No. Should I have?"

"I hear he was Helen Fainey's pimp till she gave him the boot to go freelance."

His eyes closed and opened slowly, a lazy blink. But there was nothing lazy about the mind behind those eyes.

"The hooker who got run down a few weeks ago. You were a witness."

"Right. That was Traffic Division, so I didn't know if a hooker buying it like that would make it onto your high-flying radar."

"It didn't. I checked up on you, old buddy. To see what you've been up to lately. Your name popped up in relation to the accident."

I gave him a nasty smile. "*If* it was an accident."

He rocked a while. "Is the Gus Smalley killing related in some way?"

"I don't know. Not obviously related, no. But for old times' sake? See what Tony Dyne's package has to say, would you?"

No stalling now. He reached for the phone, made his ASAP request, then sat back to rock some more.

"Either you're going to tell me," I said, "or not. I'm not gonna ask. But since it's just possible I'm onto something with this Tony Dyne character, you might want to bring me up to speed."

"Sure sounds like you're asking."

I shrugged.

The wall of tension between us was damn near palpable. Not long ago we both thought Velda had been killed and the only thing Pat and I agreed on was it was my fault. We each reacted in our own way. I crawled into a gutter and drank myself numb. Pat decided to hate me over it and finally admitted he had it bad for Velda, too. Then when she turned up alive and well, I forgave myself. He didn't.

He said, "Lou and Ricky Salem have alibis. They were at a pizza joint celebrating Ricky's wedding anniversary."

"Class all the way, the Salem boys."

"Witnesses up the wazoo. Maybe too conveniently so."

"Like if you send a hit man out to do your dirty work, it pays to be seen out and about at the time."

"Like that." He glanced at his yellow pad. "As for Gus Smalley, he was a widower. You knew that. He and his late wife Millie had two boys and a girl, all three grown, scattered to the winds—Texas, Minnesota, California. He lived alone. In three months, his pension would've kicked in. Played poker once a week and cribbage twice. Hung around at a bar where he watched sports on the weekend and bet as much as a buck at a throw."

"Big spender, old Gus. Nice life. Boring life."

Pat slapped the legal pad. "Meaning no disrespect, Gus is a dead-end in his own damn death." The gray-blue eyes zeroed in on me. "Which means this is about *you*, Mike."

I winged my arms behind my neck. "I never thought otherwise. Neither did you, old buddy. But you being a dot the t's and cross the i's sort of guy, you had to go by the book. Gus was the murder victim, so you start with who might want him dead."

"Actually . . . old buddy . . . I started with the Salem brothers. I think maybe they hired somebody to take you out." His eyes narrowed. "What do you know that I don't, Mike?"

"Oh, we really don't have time to go into all that, do we, Pat?"

"Funny as a crutch."

"All right." I sat forward. "Here's something that might make you smile. There were three tries to take me out before some bastard made Gus a dead bystander."

He stopped rocking, and I told him about the vehicular attempt, the subway theatrics, and the faked mugging.

He frowned so hard I thought the creases would stick. "And you didn't report any of this?"

"I didn't read any of it right. The first two seemed like typical big city crap. It's a dangerous town, right? The mugging, well . . . after you stick a knife in a guy's left ass cheek, you don't figure to hang around and talk to the cops about it. Even when you didn't bring the knife."

He closed his eyes. His hands closed into fists. Did he really hate me? Or maybe just hated that I'd once been his friend?

The phone rang and two tough detectives jumped a little.

"Yeah," he said into the receiver. He listened and wrote on his legal pad, nodding and saying, "Uh-huh . . . uh-huh . . . uh-huh," and finally, "Thanks."

He hung up and said, "No procuring arrests for Mr. Dyne, but that doesn't mean anything. These pimps have girls covering for them on the street and shysters covering for them in court. But he has a pretty impressive sheet."

"Give."

"Anthony J. Dyne. Twenty-nine. Lived in just about every borough, making a mark in every one. Breaking-and-entering. Assault with a deadly weapon, did a year. Three drug arrests, no convictions."

"Using or dealing?"

"Dealing. It goes on and on . . . but no pimping and only the one conviction. But there were two arrests on suspicion of murder. I can get the details to see if he sounds like a possible hit man."

I got up and yawned. "You might want to do that."

"Mike," he said softly, and there was something softer in his face, too, a remnant of a friendship gone south. "We're not kids anymore."

"I noticed."

"Can you do me a favor . . . like you said, for old times' sake? I know Gus was a pal of yours. And I know you feel responsible in a way. But for once, no wild west, okay? Just call me with what you've got."

"Where's the fun in that?"

He scowled at me and waved toward the door. "Just get out, Mike. Just get out."

The cabbie took me down to the docks and snatched up the fin I promised with a look like he was memorizing my face for when the cops checked his log book and he had to identify his fare's corpse.

The evening sky was gray and growling but I had left the trenchcoat behind and my suitcoat unbuttoned. This was the kind of sketchy gin mill where I wanted easy access to the .45 under my arm. The waterfront bouquet greeted me, salt air, grease, oil, sweat and dead fish drifting like a ghost with body odor.

If you needed to know anything about the harbor facilities stretching from the Battery to Grant's Tomb, or wanted a line on anybody in the National Maritime Union or the Teamsters, this was your port of call. If you wanted to get laid or make somebody dead, that could be arranged, too. You know the place. They have them in London and Mexico City and Rome and Hong Kong, with smaller variations in smaller locales. But none were meaner or dirtier than the bar run by Benny Joe Grissi.

The green neon GRISSI'S shorted in and out with an electric tremor above a window so filthy its glowing beer signs looked faded. A couple of miniskirt mesh-stocking whores were talking to a pair of longshoremen looking for a wet place to put it and not particular where. Compared to these girls, Helen Fainey had been a high-class call girl.

Two hardcases in old suits and new ties sat at a table just inside the door scrutinizing customers. This was not a joint for tourists and if you were the wrong color or maybe were queer or worse a cop, Grissi's got suddenly exclusive. They shot me the cop look, then remembered me from a year ago when I cleaned their clocks, and gave me timid smiles that got me grinning.

The place stunk of stale beer and sawdust, cigarette smoke floating like foul fog while a jukebox played Gene Vincent's latest hit of maybe ten years ago. The bar was along the back wall and I didn't spot my guy at the stools or the scattering of tables. The booths were arranged so you couldn't see who was sitting in them unless you went down the aisle between.

I leaned against the bar, ordered a beer and Benny Joe Grissi trundled over, his fat face smiling around his fat cigar. His voice was a sandpaper croak that went swell with his toad-like puss.

"What, are you a regular now, Mike? My boys didn't know whether to shit or piss themselves, seeing you back again."

"They could do both as far as I care."

"They ain't that coordinated."

I looked at the wide little man in the big loud tie, his belly challenging the shirt buttons under an unbuttoned orange-and-yellow plaid sportcoat that never was in style.

I said very quietly, "You know a guy named Dyne? Tony Dyne?"

"And if I say yes, what, you brace him? And my fine establishment gets turned ass-over-tea-kettle and inside out?"

My beer came. "Maybe you should consider a cover charge."

His lips were thick and wet, and his bulbous nose had an exploded look. But the tiny dark eyes in their pouches were not stupid. "If I point you to him, Mike, will you take it outside?"

"If I can."

He made an expansive gesture. "All I ask."

I put a hand on a soft shoulder with a bone poking out like a rump roast. "First, Benny Joe, tell me. Is Tony a pimp? Do his girls come around and drop off the proceeds around closing?"

The froglike face frowned. "I don't know *what* he is, but pimp? Not that I know of."

"What then?"

"Well, he's not muscle. Too wiry. Dealer, maybe. Possibly acquires things that are not rightly his. Various unsavory means toward an end. Follow?"

"Yeah." I sipped beer. "Is he a regular?"

"No, more a now-and-then. I seen him time-to-time meeting in a back booth with possible business associates discussing potential deals, I would say."

"Anything else?"

His shoulders shrugged but the rest of his body stood still. "Well, word is he's a pretty fair wheel man. That bank robbery crew last year, hitting all around the boroughs? Might have been him driving. He did some stockcar racing upstate. They say. What do I know?"

"Just everything, Benny Joe. Just everything."

He held up fat hands like a plump crossing guard. "Please try not to bust up the joint."

"Do my best."

"Last booth on the left. Back by the johns."

I finished my beer. "Got it."

The booths were packed with sailors and dock workers, drinking and laughing, some with women, hookers and cheap dates and what-have-you. And what these girls might have you didn't want.

Only one booth was home to a solitary drinker, at left next to the little hallway with the toilets. In a dark sweatshirt and jeans, he was working on a pilsner of beer in no hurry. He was medium-sized with dark brown hair just long enough to handle the sideburns. His eyes were brown, crowding his aquiline nose, and his teeth were slightly bucked. He was in his late twenties but his cheeks were still freckled with acne.

He was my mugger.

He was also Tony Dyne.

The guy I came here to talk to.

But he was in no mood to talk, judging by how seeing me he immediately abandoned his beer to go wide-eyed scrambling out of the booth and heading down toward the end of the hallway where the red EXIT sign glowed. I caught him before he got there and flung him through a door optimistically marked GENTLEMEN. He went flying into and through the door of the only enclosed stall and sat down there, jarringly. Two guys at the urinals finished up and went out without looking at us or washing their hands, either.

Benny Joe came blustering in, saying, "Mike, Mike, damnit boy, I *told* you—"

41

"Put a 'Closed for Cleaning' sign on the door, Benny Joe."

"I don't have one!"

"Then hang an 'Out-of-Order!' And get lost."

He sighed, shook his head, but went out.

It smelled like you'd expect, excrement, urine and puke fighting for dominance. The floor was filthy enough to be modern art. The washstand looked like something leaned against the wall waiting to be thrown out, and the mirror was a smeary thing reflective of nothing at all.

He was shaking. At first I thought he was in need of a fix. But he was no druggie. No longhair wig tonight, either. He was just flat-out scared shitless.

"Three times you tried to kill me, Tony. Why?"

He played no games. No denials at all.

"I knew you were comin' after me! *Everybody* knows about you. Everybody knows what you do to people."

"I wasn't coming after you, Tony."

His eyes were wild, upper lip quivering over the bucked teeth. "You're *here*, ain't you?"

"I'm here. Because you killed that old guy in the lobby of the Hackard Building."

He was shaking his head, but it didn't mean "no." "I . . . I . . . *hell*, man, I just lost my cool. I thought you'd be there and you wasn't and he starts asking questions and got loud and . . ."

"And you shot him."

He nodded. The close-set eyes looked sorry. "Didn't mean to, man."

"Who hired you?"

"Hired me? *Nobody* hired me. I *told* you. Night after night, you went walking past where that hooker died."

"How did you know I did that?"

"Your name . . . it was in the papers. Little squib on the accident, but your name jumped out at me. So I . . . started following you."

"I never saw you."

"I'm good at it. Mostly it was in a car. Different car every night."

"You'd boost a different car every night. Just to follow me?"

He nodded. His tongue curved around the buck teeth. "Worked, didn't it? And I was right, wasn't I? Here you are!"

"Take it easy. Now. Who hired you?"

"I *told* you—"

I slapped him. "Not to kill me. To kill Helen Fainey."

"Oh. Her."

"Yeah. Her."

He swallowed. His cheek was red. Then he spilled in a rush of words that would have challenged a court reporter.

"A guy named Clifford. Lawrence Clifford. He's from Nebraska, Omaha, but he does lots of business in New York. Insurance or something. You know, married guy, likes to fool around. I guess he took a shine to this Fainey bitch. Got to seeing her regular when he come to town. Then maybe she tried to blackmail him or some crap. I dunno. He wanted her gone."

I pointed toward the bar. "You arranged it here, didn't you? Right out in that booth."

His eyes were wide under a furrowed brow. "That's right. How did *you* know?"

"How much did he pay?"

"A grand. Cash."

I slapped him again.

"What the hell was *that* for, man?"

"Just for me, Tony. You were supposed to meet Clifford here tonight, right?"

He frowned at me, studying me like I was a witch. "How do you *know* this shit?"

"Why were you meeting him, Tony?"

"I . . . I told him I needed more money. I needed to get out of town."

"Why?"

His eyes widened again and his upper lip curled back over the bucked teeth. "Why do you *think*? Because Mike Hammer was on my ass! Get real!"

That was when he sprang.

Leapt right at me and took us both from the stall and I went backward, balance gone, hitting my tailbone on the floor and my head on the washstand pillar. Stunned, I heard the click and then he was over me, grinning like a demented surgeon, the blade the only gleaming thing in this dingy chamber. His hand with the knife moved and my knee drove his balls up into him and as he crumpled in two, screeching in pain, I grabbed him by the wrist and swung his hand with the blade into himself with a sickening squish and put everything into it as I swung the sunk-in blade around in an uneven circle that opened his stomach up and let him reconsider what he had for supper.

I got to my feet, breathing hard. Hardly any gore on me. On the back of my head a bump was rising, but it wasn't wet with blood.

Tony Dyne lay sprawled on the grimy floor, his guts spilled out.

Benny Joe pushed his way in and his expression was tragic. Somehow his men's room had managed to get nastier. "Mike, Mike, boy, what have you *done*?"

"I kept it in here, didn't I? You got a phone I can use? I need to call Captain Chambers of Homicide."

The fat face fought hysteria. "The cops? *Why*, Mike? I can take care of this for you."

"You're a pal, Benny Joe, but I need to do this the right way. Better leave the 'Out of Order' sign on the door a while."

We both stepped out. Grissi was shaking his head. He looked like he'd lost his best friend.

"This is gonna be so bad for business."

"A killing?"

"No! Having cops in the place."

At a phone brought out from under the counter, I called Pat and told him where to send his team, asking him to come personally.

"I wouldn't miss it," he said sourly and hung up.

This time Pat got there before the forensics team. He looked around at the dismal, emptied-out bar and said, "Glad you found a new regular hang-out, Mike. Puts the Blue Ribbon to shame."

"Save the sarcasm," I said.

I walked him to the men's room and explained in broad strokes what had happened.

"I'm not surprised," Pat said, nodding down at the dead man. "He killed Gus and you killed him."

"Hey, I was going to hand him over to you. As a kind of olive branch. But the guy jumped me. With a knife. What could I do?"

"Help him disembowel himself, apparently."

Now the forensics crew came and we made way for them, stepping back out into the now-empty bar. A plainclothes guy was interviewing an obsequious Benny Joe Grissi.

"Okay, Pat," I said. "I'm going to prove myself to you. I'm going to give you a killer, and I'm not even coming along."

He grunted half a laugh. "This should be good."

"It is good. The guy who hired the late Tony Dyne to run down Helen Fainey is a Nebraska businessman named Lawrence Clifford."

I shared with Pat what Velda had dug up for me, including that our insurance contacts confirmed Tony Dyne as a suspected expert in staging vehicular accidents. And also that the "most successful ad agency in the Tri-State area" didn't exist, among other interesting facts about our client. No wonder he'd paid me in cash.

Like he had Tony Dyne.

"You'll find Clifford at the New Yorker Hotel," I told him. "Registered as Andrew Fainey."

He frowned. "*Fainey*?"

"Clifford came around to my office this morning pretending to be Helen's father."

I gave him chapter and verse.

"You saw through him right away?" Pat asked.

"No, but enough to have Vel call around on him." I shrugged. "The guy said himself that the story of his daughter was an old one, and he was way too vague—hell, he didn't know the name of the detective hired to find his daughter's killer!"

"But he knew *your* name all right." There was some sneer in his smile. "Your reputation precedes you."

"I guess it does. I think he arranged for me to meet up with Tony Dyne tonight to kill his ass . . ."

"Which you did."

". . . or maybe vice versa, which would've worked out almost as well for him. But I think he figured I'd prevail and all his problems would vanish."

Pat was thinking about it. "With Dyne dead, I wonder if we'll have enough to put Clifford away."

I put a hand on his shoulder. "I can't do your whole job for you, chum. I'll testify to what Dyne told me before he died. Should be enough."

"And if it isn't?"

"Don't tempt me."

And Pat Chambers shook his head and laughed.

A LONG TIME DEAD

Kratch was dead.

They ran forty thousand volts through him in the stone mansion called Rahway State Prison with eight witnesses in attendance to watch him strain against the straps and smoke until his heart had stopped and his mind quit functioning.

An autopsy had opened his body to visual inspection and all his parts had been laid out on a table, probed and pored over, then slopped back in the assorted cavities and sewn shut with large economical stitches.

One old aunt, his mother's sister, came forth to claim the remains and, with what little she had, treated him to a funeral. Kratch had left a fortune but it was tied up, and auntie was on his mother's side of the family, and poor—Dad had married a succession of showgirls, and Kratch's mom had been the only one to produce an heir.

Whether hoping for a bequest or out of a sense of decency her nephew hadn't inherited, the old girl sat beside the coffin for two days and two nights, moving only to replace the candles when they burned down. Her next-door neighbor brought her the occasional plate of food, crying softly because nobody else had come to this wake.

Just before the hearse arrived, a small man carrying a camera entered the room, smiled at the old lady, offered his condolences and asked if he could take a picture of the infamous departed.

There was no objection.

Quietly, he moved around the inexpensive wooden coffin, snapped four shots with a 35MM Nikon, thanked auntie and left. The next day the news service carried a sharp, clear photo of the notorious Grant Kratch, even to the stitches where they had slid his scalp back after taking off the top of his head on the autopsy table.

No doubt about it.

Kratch was dead.

The serial killer who had sent at least thirty-seven sexually defiled young women to early graves was nothing more than a compost pile himself now.

It had been a pleasure to nail that bastard. I had wanted to kill him when I found him, but the chance that he might give up information during interrogation that would bring some peace of mind to dozens of loved ones out there made me restrain myself.

I knew it was a risk—he was a rich kid who had inherited enough loot to bribe his way out of about anything—but I figured the papers would play up the horror show of the bodies buried on his Long Island estate and keep corruption at bay.

So I'd dragged him into the Fourth Precinct Station, let the cops have him, then sat through the trial where he got the death penalty, sweated out the appeal lest some soft-hearted judge drop it to a life sentence, then was a witness to his smoldering contortions in the big oaken hot seat.

Oh, Kratch was dead all right.

Then what was he doing on a sunny Spring afternoon, getting into a taxicab outside the Eastern terminal at LaGuardia Airport?

Damn. I felt like I was in an acid dropper's kaleidoscope—it came fast, so fast, no warning . . . just a slow turn of the head and there he was, thirty feet away, a big man in a Brooks Brothers suit with a craggily handsome face whose perversity exposed itself only in his eyes, and the hate wrenched at my stomach and I could taste the bitterness of vomit. I had my hand on the butt of the .45 and almost yanked it out of the jacket when my reflexes caught hold and froze me to the spot.

Those same reflexes kept me out of his line of sight while my mind detailed every inch of him. He wasn't trying to hide. He wasn't doing a damn thing except standing there waiting for a taxi to pick him up. When one came, he told the cabbie to take him to the Commodore and the voice he spoke in was Kratch's voice.

And Kratch was a long time dead.

I flagged down the next cab and told the driver to take me to the Commodore, and gave him the route I wanted. All he had to do was look at my face and he knew something was hot and leaned into the job. I was forty-five seconds behind Kratch at the terminal, but I was waiting in the Commodore lobby a full five minutes before he came in.

At the desk he said his name was Grossman and they put him on the sixth floor. I got to the elevator bank before he did, went up to the sixth and waited out of sight until he got out and walked away. When he'd gone in his room, I eased past it and noted the number—620.

Downstairs I asked for something on the sixth, got 601, then went up to my room and sat down to try to put a wild fifty minutes into focus.

There are some things so highly improbable that any time considering them is wasted time. All I knew was that I had just seen Kratch and that the son of a bitch was a long time dead. So that put a lookalike on the scene—a possible twin or a relative with an exceptional resemblance.

Bullshit.

That *was* Kratch I saw. Not unless they had developed human clones, after all. I looked around the room I'd laid down eighty bucks for, wondering just what I had been thinking about when I registered. Been a long while since I'd taken off half-cocked on a dead run like this and I had damned near pushed myself into a corner.

Great plan I had—push his door button, then pull a gun on him, walk inside and do a dance on his head—maybe I'd pop those autopsy stitches. Only if I had the wrong guy my ass was grass. I'd had to drop a credit card at the registry desk and a halfway decent description would point a finger right at me.

Aside from a dead guy who was up and walking around, the basic situation wasn't a new one—I wanted to look around somebody else's hotel room. And after a lot of years in the private cop business in New York, I had plenty of options, legal and ill. I propped my door open enough to see anybody who might pass by, then dialed the Spider's number and got his terse, "Yeah?"

"Mike Hammer, kid."

It had been more than a year since I'd seen him, so I got a special greeting: "Whaddya want?"

"That gimmick you use for not letting a hotel door shut all the way."

"You goin' inta my business?"

"Don't get smart."

"Where are you?"

"The Commodore."

"And you can't rig something up your own self? Hell, you got wire in the furniture, and in the toilet bowl—"

"Look, I haven't got time. Just bring it over."

"Give me till tonight and I'll get you a passkey."

"No. Now."

"Mike—cut a guy a break. Security knows me there."

"Then send Billy. I'm in 601."

"You're a pain in the ass, Mike."

"Tell me that when yours is back in the can again."

"Okay." He let out a sigh that was meant for me to hear. "This better even up the books."

"Not hardly. But it's a start."

Twenty minutes later, Billy Chappey, looking like the original preppie, showed up at my door to hand me a small envelope, winked knowingly and strutted off. He sure didn't look like one of the best safe-crackers in the city.

After three tries on my own door, I had the routine down pat. Once it was in place, the little spring-loaded gimmick was hardly noticeable. I eased out into the hall, walked down to room 620, slipped the gizmo into the proper spot, then went back to my room again.

After two rings, he answered the phone with a pleasant, resonant, "Hello?" He sounded curious but not at all anxious.

I put something nasal in my voice. "Mr. Grossman?"

"Yes."

"This is the front desk, sir. When we entered your credit card in our machine, there was a malfunction and the printout was illegible. Strictly our problem, but would it be too much trouble for you to come down and let us do it over?"

"Not at all. I'll be there right away."

"Thank you. The management would like to send a complimentary drink to your room for the inconvenience."

"That's nice of you. Make it a martini. Very dry."

"Yes. Certainly, sir."

He was punctual, all right. His feet came by my door, and I waited until the elevator opened and shut, then went to his room and went the hell on in. Wouldn't be time to shake the place down. All I wanted was one thing and I lucked out: he had used the water glass in the bathroom and his prints were all over it. I replaced it with one from my room, after wetting it down, then took the gimmick off the door, which I let close behind me.

The hall was still empty when I shut myself up in my own room. I pulled the bed covers down, messed up the sheets, punched a dent in the pillow and hung a DO NOT DISTURB sign on the door knob.

When I got to the lobby, the guy calling himself Grossman was just leaving the bell desk with two no-nonsense security types. They both wore frozen expressions, having been through countless scam situations before. Grossman's face seemed to say someone was playing a joke on him, and nothing more.

My pal Pat Chambers was Captain of Homicide and couldn't be bothered with chasing wild gooses.

"No it's *not* Grant Kratch's print," he growled at me over the phone, after running the errand for me. "Jesus, Mike, that guy is dead as hell!"

"I wish I'd made him that way. Then I could be sure."

"The print belongs to Arnold Veslo, a smalltime hood who hasn't been in trouble with the law since the mid-fifties."

"What kind of smalltime hood, Pat?"

"He had a couple of local busts for burglary, then turned up as a wheelman for Cootie Banners in Trenton. Did a little time and dropped off the face of the earth."

"Dropped off the face of the earth when? About the time the state fried Kratch?"

"I guess. So what?"

"Messenger over Veslo's photo and anything you got on him."

"Oh, well, sure! We aim to please, Mr. Hammer!"

"I pay my taxes," I said, and hung up on him.

Velda had been eavesdropping from the doorway, but now the big beautiful brunette swung her hips into my inner sanctum, pulled up the client's chair and filled it, crossing long, lovely legs. She could turn a simple white blouse and black skirt into a public decency beef.

"You want me to start checking on this Arnold Veslo?"

I shook my head. "We'll wait and see what Pat sends over. What about the aunt?"

Most people thought Velda was my secretary. They were right, as far as it went—but she was also the other licensed P.I. in this office, and my partner. In various ways.

"Long time dead," she said. "Some bitterness about that in the old neighborhood—seems Kratch didn't leave the old lady a dime."

I was trying to get a Lucky going with the desk lighter. She got up, thumbed it to life with one try, and lit me up. "Sure you aren't seeing ghosts?"

"Once I've killed this guy—*really* killed him—then maybe I'll see a ghost."

She settled her lovely fanny on the edge of my desk, folded her arms over the impressive shelf of her bosom, and the lush, luscious mouth curled into a catlike smile. "That all it takes to get a death sentence out of you, Mike? Just resemble some long-gone killer?"

I grinned at her through drifting smoke. "That was Kratch, all right, doll. And I don't think there was anything supernatural about it."

I'd already filled her in on what I'd got at the Commodore. It wasn't the kind of hotel where engravings of George Washington could get you much information. But Abraham Lincoln still had a following.

"So you're stalking an insurance salesman from Lincoln, Nebraska," she said, her mouth amused but her eyes worried, "in the big city for a convention."

"Not just a salesman. He has his own agency. And he'll be here through Sunday. So we've got a couple days. And I hung onto my room on the sixth floor. So I have a base of operations."

"So there's no rush killing him, then."

"Shut up."

"Remind me how this pays the overhead again?"

"Some things," I said, "a guy has to do just to feel good about himself."

The file Pat sent over on Arnold Veslo seemed an immediate dead end. During the war, young Veslo had been tossed out of the army for getting drunk and beating up an officer. As Pat indicated on the phone, the lowlife's stellar postwar career ran from burglary to assault, and notes indicated he'd been connected to Cootie Banner, part of a home invasion crew whose members were all either dead or in stir.

But where was Veslo now?

If that fingerprint was to be believed, he was an insurance broker named Grossman staying at the Commodore. But as far as the states of New York and New Jersey knew, Veslo had been released from Rahway a dozen years ago and done a disappearing act.

This time I was in Velda's domain, the outer office, sitting on the edge of her desk, which visually doesn't stack up with her sitting on the edge of my desk, but you can't have everything. I was studying the Veslo file.

"I can't find any connection," I said. "But I do have a hunch."

She rolled her eyes. "Rarely a good sign. . . ."

"Stay with me." I showed her the mug shots. "You remember what Kratch looked like, right? Would you say this guy bears a resemblance?"

She squinted at the front-and-side photos I was dangling. "Not really."

"Look past the big nose and the bushy eyebrows. Check out the bone structure."

"Well . . . yeah. It's there, I suppose. What, plastic surgery?"

I shrugged. "Kratch had dough up the wazoo. It's Hollywood bullshit that you can turn anybody into anybody else, under the knife—but if you start out with a resemblance, and the facial underpinning is right . . ."

"Maybe," she said with a grudging nod. "But so what? You aren't seriously suggesting a scenario where Kratch hires Veslo to undergo plastic surgery, and then . . . take his place?"

"Kratch had enough dough to pull just about anything off."

For as beautiful as she was, she could serve up an ugly smirk. "Sure. Makes great sense. Here's a million bucks, pal—all you gotta do is die for me. And by the way, let's trade fingerprints!"

"There are only two places in the system where fingerprint cards would need switching—Central Headquarters and the prison itself—and suddenly Kratch's new swirls are Veslo's old ones."

She frowned in thought. "Just bribe a couple of clerks. . . . It *could* be done. So what now, Mike?"

"Doll," I said, sliding off the desk onto the floor, "I got things I want you to check out—you'll need the private detective's chief weapon to do it, though."

"What, a .45? You know I pack a .38."

"That's an understatement." I patted the phone on the desk. "Here's your weapon. You walk your fingers. Mike has to follow his nose."

I told her what I wanted done, retrieved my hat from the closet and headed out.

George at the Blue Ribbon on Forty-fourth Street had a habit of hiring ex-cops for bartenders. It wasn't a rough joint by any means, in fact a classy German restaurant with a bar decorated by signed celebrity photos and usually some of the celebrities who signed them. Still, a bar is a bar and having aprons who could handle themselves always came in handy.

Lou Berwicki was in his mid-sixties, and worked afternoons, six-two of muscle and bone and gristle, with a bucket head, stubbly gray hair and ice-blue eyes that missed nothing.

He was also an ex-cellblock guard from Rahway State Prison.

Lou got off at four-thirty, and I was waiting for him at my

usual table in a nook around a corner. I had ordered us both beers and, as his last duty of the shift, he brought them over.

We shook. He had one of those beefy paws your hand can get lost in, even a mitt like mine.

"Great to see you, Lou."

"Stuff it, Mike—I can tell by that shit-eating grin, this is business. What the hell can an old warhorse like me do to help a young punk like you?"

I liked guys in their sixties. They thought guys in their thirties were young.

I said, "I need to thumb through your memory book, Lou. Need some info about Rahway, and I hate driving to New Jersey."

"Who doesn't?"

"You didn't work Death Row."

"Hell no. My God, it was depressing enough on the main cellblocks."

"But you knew the guys who did?"

"Yeah. Knew everybody there. Big place, small staff—we all knew each other. Paid to. What's this about?"

I lighted up a smoke; took some in, let some out. "About ten years ago they gave Grant Kratch the hot squat."

"Couldn't happen to a nicer guy."

"How well did you know the bulls working that block?"

"Enough, I guess. What's this about, Mike?"

"Any rotten apples?"

He shrugged. "You know how it is. Prison pay stinks. So there's always guys willing to do favors."

"How about a *big* favor?"

"Don't follow. . . ."

"I have a wild hair up my ass, Lou. You may need another beer to follow this. . . ."

"Try me."

"Say a guy comes to visit Kratch, maybe the day before he's set to take the electric cure. This guy maybe comes in as Kratch's lawyer—might be he's in a beard and glasses and wig."

"I think I *will* have that beer . . ." Lou gulped the rest of his down, and waved a waitress over. "I didn't know you were still readin' comic books, Mike."

"Hear me out. Say this guy has had plastic surgery and is now a ringer for Kratch—"

"This may take a boilermaker."

"So they switch clothes, and Kratch walks, and the ringer gets the juice."

Lou shook his head, laughed without humor. "It's a fairy tale, Mike. Who would do that? Who would take a guy's place in the hot seat?"

"Maybe somebody with cancer or some other incurable disease. Somebody who has family he wants taken care of. Remember that guy in Miami, who popped Cermak for the Capone crowd? He had cancer of the stomach."

The old ex-prison guard was well into the second beer now. Maybe that was why he said, "Okay. So what you're saying is, could you pull that off with the help of the right bent screw?"

"That's what I'm saying. Was anybody working on Death Row at that time that could have been bought? And we're talking big money, Lou—Irish sweepstakes money."

The beer froze halfway from the table to his face. Lou was a pale guy naturally but he went paler.

"Shit," he said. "Conrad."

"Who?"

"Jack Conrad. He was only about fifty, but he took early retirement. The word was, he'd inherited dough. He went to Florida. Him and his wife and kids."

"He was crooked?"

"Everybody knew he was the guy selling booze and cigarettes to the inmates. Legend has it he snuck women in. Whether that's true or not, I can't tell you. But I *can* tell you something that'll curl your hair."

"Go, man."

He leaned forward. "Somebody *murdered* Conrad—maybe . . . a year after he moved down there. Murdered him and his whole family. He had a nice-looking teenage daughter who got raped in the bargain. Real nasty shit, man."

I was smiling.

"Jesus, Mike—I tell you a horror story and you start grinning. What's wrong with you?"

"Maybe I know something you don't."

"Yeah, what?"

"That the story might have a happy ending."

Velda was in the client's chair again, but her legs weren't crossed—her feet were on the floor and her knees together. Prim as a schoolmarm.

"How did you know?" she asked.

"I said it was a hunch."

She was pale as death, after hearing what Lou had shared with me.

"Arnold Veslo had a good-looking wife and child, a young boy," she said, reporting what she'd discovered. "Two weeks after Kratch was executed, Mrs. Veslo was found at home—

raped and murdered. The boy's neck was snapped. No one was ever brought to justice. What kind of monster—"

"You know what kind."

She leaned in and tapped the fat file folder on my desk. "Like you asked, I checked our file on Veslo—it's mostly clippings, but there's a lot of them. And I put the key one on top."

I flipped the folder open, and they stared back at me, both of them—Arnold Veslo and Grant Kratch. Veslo in a chauffeur's cap and uniform, opening the car door for his employer, Kratch, who'd been brought in for questioning two weeks before I hauled his ass and the necessary evidence into the Fourth Precinct.

"You were right," she said, rapping a knuckle on the yellowed newsprint. "Veslo worked for Kratch. How did you know? What are you, psychic?"

"No. I'm not even smart. But I saw a murderer today, a living, breathing one, and I knew there had to be a way."

She shrugged. "So we bring Pat in, right? You lay it all out, and the investigation begins. If Grossman really is Kratch, then before his 'death,' Kratch had to find a way to transfer his estate into some kind of bank setup where his new identity could access it. That kind of thing can be traced. You can get this guy, Mike."

"Velda, we know for sure Kratch killed and raped thirty-seven women over a five-year period. Mostly prostitutes and runaways. You remember our clients' faces? The parents of the last girl?"

She swallowed and nodded.

"Well, it's a damn sure bet that he also killed that prison guard's family *and* Veslo's, and got his jollies with a couple more sexual assaults along the way. And do you really think that's his whole damn tally?"

"What do you mean, Mike?"

"I mean 'Grossman' has spent the last ten years doing more than selling insurance, you can damn well bet. Think about it—you just *know* there are missing women in unmarked graves all across the heartland."

"God," she said, ashen. "How many more has he killed?"

"No one but that sick bastard knows. But you can be sure of one thing, doll."

"What?"

"There won't be any more."

Back in my hotel room, I was still weighing exactly how I wanted to play this. I'd been seen here, and a few people knew I'd been asking about Grossman, so even if I handled this with care, I'd probably get hauled in for questioning.

And of course Captain Pat Chambers already knew the basics of the situation.

With my door open, and me sitting in a chair with my back to the wall, I had a concealed view of the hallway. I wasn't even sure Kratch was in his room. I was considering going down there, and using the passkey I'd taken Spider up on, and just taking my chances confronting the bastard. I'd rigged self-defense pleas before.

Which was the problem. I was a repeat offender in that department, and the right judge could get frisky.

I was mulling this when the bellboy brought the cute little prostitute—because that's surely what she was—up to the door of 620. She had curly blonde Annie hair and a sparkly blue minidress and looked about sixteen.

I could see Kratch, in a white terry cloth Commodore robe, slip into the hall, give the bellboy a twenty, pat him on the shoulder, send him on his way, pat the prostitute on the bottom, and guide her in.

Knowing Kratch's sexual proclivities, I didn't feel I had much choice but to intervene. My .45 was tucked in the speed rig under my sport jacket, the passkey in my hand. It was about ten p.m. and traffic in the hall was scant—too late for people to be heading out, too early for them to be coming back.

So I stood by that door and listened. I could hear them in there talking. He was smooth, with a resonant baritone, very charming. She sounded young and a little high. Whether drugs or booze, I couldn't tell you.

Then it got quiet, and that worried me.

What the hell, I thought, and I used the passkey.

I got lucky—they were in the bathroom. The door was cracked and I could hear his smooth banter and her girlish giggling, a radio going, some middle-of-the-road station playing romantic strings, mixed with the bubbling rumble of a Jacuzzi.

I got the .45 out and helped myself to a real look around, this time—this was a suite, a sprawl of luxury. There was a wet bar and I could see where he'd made drinks for them. In back of the bar, I found the pill bottle, and a sniff of a lipstick-kissed glass told me the bastard had slipped her a mickey.

That wasn't the most fun thing he had in store for her—I checked the three big suitcases, and one had clothes, and another had toys. You know the kind—handcuffs and whips and chains and assorted S & M goodies. Nothing was in the last big, oversize suitcase.

Not yet.

So he had a whole evening planned for her, didn't he? But there's always a party pooper in the crowd. . . .

When I burst into the bathroom with the .45 in hand, he

and his big hard piston practically jumped out of the big deep tub. The hot bubbles were going, and more drinks sat on the edge of the tub, but I motioned with the gun for him to sit down and stay put. The girl didn't notice me, or anyway didn't notice me much. She was half-unconscious already, leaning back against the tub, a sweet little nude with hooded eyes and pert handfuls with tiny tips poking up out of the froth like flowers just starting to grow.

I held the gun on him as he frowned at me in seeming incomprehension and I leaned over and lifted the girl by a skinny arm out of the tub. She didn't seem to mind. She might have been a child of twelve but for the cupcake breasts. If I hadn't got here when I did, she wouldn't have ever got any older.

She managed to stand on wobbly feet, her wet feet slippery on the tile.

I took her chin in my free hand. "I'm the cops. You want to leave. Wake up! This bastard doped you."

Life leapt into her eyes, and self-preservation kicked in, and she stumbled into the other room. I left the door open as I trained the gun on Kratch.

He was a handsome guy, as far as it went. His hair was gray and in tight Roman curls, with a pockmarked ruggedness, his chest hair going white, too, stark on tanned flesh. His erection had wilted. Having a .45 pointed at you will do that.

And he frowned at me, as if I were just some deranged intruder—he didn't have to fake the fear.

"My name is Grossman. I'm an insurance salesman from Nebraska. Take my money from my wallet—it's by the bed. You can have it all. Just don't hurt the girl."

That made me laugh.

She stuck her head in. She was dressed now. Didn't take long with those skimpy threads.

"Thank you, mister," she said.

"I never saw you," I said. "And you never saw me."

She nodded prettily and was out of the door.

I grinned at him. "Alone at last. Are you really going to play games, Kratch?"

He smiled. "Almost didn't recognize you, Hammer. You're not as young as you used to be."

"No, but I can still recognize a piece of shit when I see one."

"No one else will. I'm a respectable citizen. Have been for a long, long time."

"I don't think so. I think Grossman is just the latest front for your sick appetites. How many young girls like that have you raped and killed in the past ten years or so, Kratch? I will go to my grave regretting I didn't kill you the first time around."

"My name isn't Kratch." The fear had ebbed. He had an oily confidence—if I was going to kill him, he figured, I'd have done it by now. "It's Grossman. And you will never prove otherwise. You can put all your resources and connections behind it, Hammer, and you will never, *ever* have the proof you need."

"Since when did I give a damn about proof?"

The radio made a simple splash going in, like a big bar of soap, and he did not scream or thrash, simply froze with clawed hands and a look of horror that had come over him as the deadly little box came sailing his way. I held the plug in and let the juice have him and endured the sick smell of scorched flesh with no idea whether he could feel what I was seeing, the all-over blisters forming like so many more bubbles, the hair on his head catching fire like a flaming hat, fingertips bursting like overdone sausages, eyes bulging, then popping, one two, *like plump squeezed grapes, leaving sightless black sockets crying scarlet tears as he cooked in the gravy of his own gore.*

I unplugged the thing, and the grotesque corpse slipped under the roiling water.

"*Now* you're fucking dead," I said.

GRAVE MATTER

If I hadn't been angry, I wouldn't have been driving so damn fast, and if I hadn't been driving so damn fast, in a lashing rain, on a night so dark closing your eyes made no difference, my high beams a pitiful pair of flashlights trying to guide the way in the vast cavern of the night, illuminating only slashes of storm, I would have had time to brake properly, when I came down over the hill and saw, in a sudden white strobe of electricity, that the bridge was gone, or anyway out of sight, somewhere down there under the rush of rain-raised river, and when the brakes didn't take, I yanked the wheel around and my heap was sideways in a flooded ditch, wheels spinning. Like my head.

I got out on the driver's side, because otherwise I would have had to swim underwater. From my sideways tipped car, I leapt to the slick highway, as rain pelted me mercilessly, and did a fancy slip-slide dance keeping my footing. Then I snugged the wings of the trenchcoat collar up around my face and began to walk back the way I'd come. If rain was God's tears, the Old Boy sure was bawling about something tonight.

I knew how he felt. I'd spent the afternoon in the upstate burg of Hopeful, only there was nothing hopeful about the sorry little hamlet. All I'd wanted was a few answers to a few questions. Like how a guy who won a Silver Star charging up a beachhead could wind up a crushed corpse in a public park, a crumpled piece of discarded human refuse.

Bill Reynolds had had his problems. Before the war he'd been an auto mechanic in Hopeful. A good-looking dark-haired bruiser who'd have landed a football scholarship if the war hadn't got in the way, Bill married his high school sweet-heart before he shipped out, only when he came back missing an arm and a leg, he found his girl wasn't interested in what was left of him. Even though he was good with his prosthetic arm and leg, he couldn't get his job back at the garage, either.

But the last time I'd spoken to Bill, when he came in to New York to catch Marciano and Jersey Joe at Madison Square Garden, he'd said things were looking up. He said he had a handy-man job lined up, and that it was going to pay better than his old job at the garage.

"Besides which," he said, between rounds, "you oughta see my boss. You'd do overtime yourself."

"You mean you're working for a woman?"

"And what a woman. She's got more curves than Storm King Mountain road."

"Easy you don't drive off a cliff."

That's all we'd said about the subject, because Marciano had come out swinging at that point, and the next I heard from Bill—well not from him, *about* him—he was dead.

The only family he had left in Hopeful was a maiden aunt; she called me collect, and told me tearfully that Bill's body had been found in the city park. His spine had been snapped.

"How does a thing like that happen, Chief?"

Chief Thadeous Dolbert was one of Hopeful's four full-time cops. Despite his high office, he wore a blue uniform indistinguishable from his underlings, and his desk was out in the open of the little bullpen in Hopeful City Hall. A two-cell lockup was against one wall, and spring sunshine streaming in the windows through the bars sent slanting stripes of shadow across his desk and his fat florid face. He was leaning back in his swivel chair, eyes hooded; he looked like a fat iguana—I expected his tongue to flick out and capture a fly any second now.

Dolbert said, "We figure he got hit by a car."

"Body was found in the city park, wasn't it?"

"Way he was bunged up, figure he must've got whopped a good one, really sent him flyin'."

"Was that the finding at the inquest?"

Dolbert fished a pack of cigarettes out of his breast pocket, right behind his tarnished badge; lighted himself up a smoke. Soon it was dangling from a thick slobber-flecked lower lip. "We don't stand much on ceremony around here, mister. County coroner called it accidental death at the scene."

"That's all the investigation Bill's death got?"

Dolbert shrugged, blew a smoke circle. "All that was warranted."

I sat forward. "All that was warranted. A local boy, who gave an arm and a leg to his country, wins a damn Silver Star doin' it, and you figure him getting his spine snapped like a twig and damn near every bone in his body broken, well that's just pretty much business as usual here in Hopeful."

Under the heavy lids, fire flared in the fat chief's eyes. "You think you knew Bill Reynolds? You knew the old Bill. You didn't know the drunken stumblebum he turned into. Prime candidate for stepping out in front of a car."

"I never knew Bill to drink to excess . . ."

"How much time did you spend with him, lately?"

A hot rush of shame crawled up my neck. I'd seen Bill from time to time, in the city, when he came in to see me; but I'd never come up to Hopeful. Never really gone out of my way for him, since the war . . .

Till now.

"You make any effort to find the hit-and-run driver that did this?"

The chief shrugged. "Nobody saw it happen."

"You don't even know for sure a car did it."

"How the hell else could it have happened?"

I stood up, pushed back, the legs of my wooden chair scraping the hard floor like fingernails on a blackboard. "That's what I'm going to find out."

A finger as thick as a pool cue waggled at me. "You got no business stickin' your damn nose in around here, Hammer—"

"I'm a licensed investigator in the state of New York, Pops. And I'm working for Bill Reynolds' aunt."

He snorted a laugh. "Working for that senile old biddy? She's out at the county hospital. She's broke! Couldn't even afford a damn funeral . . . we had to bury the boy in potter's field . . ."

That was one of Hopeful's claims to fame: the state buried its unknown, unclaimed, impoverished dead, in the potter's field here.

"Why didn't you tell Uncle Sam?" I demanded. "Bill was a war hero—they'd've put him in Arlington . . ."

Dolbert shrugged. "Not my job."

"What the hell *is* your job?"

"Watch your mouth, city boy." He nodded toward the holding cells and the cigarette quivered as the fat mouth sneered. "Don't forget you're in *my* world . . ."

Maybe Bill Reynolds didn't get a funeral, or a gravestone; but he was going to get a memorial by way of an investigation.

Only nobody in Hopeful wanted to talk to me. The supposed "accident" had occurred in the middle of the night, and my only chance for a possible witness was in the all-night diner across from the Civil War cannon in the park.

The diner's manager, a skinny character with a horsey face darkened by perpetual five o'clock shadow, wore a grease-stained apron over his grease-stained tee-shirt. Like the chief, he had a cigarette drooping from slack lips. The ash narrowly missed falling into the cup of coffee he'd served me as I sat at the counter with half a dozen locals.

"We got a jukebox, mister," the manager said. "Lots of kids end up here, tail end of a Saturday night. That was a Saturday night, when Bill got it, ya know? That loud music, joint jumpin', there coulda been a train wreck out there and nobody'da heard it."

"Nobody would have seen an accident, out your windows?"

The manager shrugged. "Maybe ol' Bill got hit on the other side of the park."

But it was just a little square of grass and benches and such; the "other side of the park" was easily visible from the windows lining the diner booths—even factoring in the grease and lettering.

I talked to a couple of waitresses, who claimed not to have been working that night. One of them, "Gladys" her name tag said, a heavyset bleached blonde who must have been pretty cute twenty years ago, served me a slice of apple pie and cheese and a piece of information.

"Bill said he was going to work as a handyman," I said, "for some good-lookin' gal. You know who that would've been?"

"Sure," Gladys said. She had sky-blue eyes and nicotine-yellow teeth. "He was working out at the mansion."

"The what?"

"The mansion. The old Riddle place. You must've passed it on the highway, comin' in to town."

"I saw a gate and a drive, and got a glimpse of a big old gothic brick barn . . ."

She nodded, refilled my coffee. "That's the one. The Riddles, they owned this town forever. Ain't a building downtown that the Riddles ain't owned since the dawn of time. But Mr. Riddle, he was the last of the line, and he and his wife died in that plane crash, oh, ten years ago. The only one left now is the daughter, Victoria."

"What was Bill doing out at the Riddle place?"

She shrugged. "Who knows? Who cares? Maybe Miz Riddle just wanted some company. Bill was still a handsome so and so, even minus a limb or two. He coulda put his shoe under my bed anytime."

"Victoria Riddle isn't married? She lives alone?"

"Alone except for that hairless ape."

"What?"

"She's got a sort of butler, you know, a servant? He was her father's chauffeur. Big guy. Mute. Comes in to town, does the grocery shopping and such. We hardly ever see Miz Riddle, 'less she's meeting with her lawyer, or going to the bank to visit all her money."

"What does she do out there?"

"Who knows? She's not interested in business. Her daddy, he had his finger in every pie around here. Miz Riddle, she lets her lawyer run things and I guess the family money, uh, under-what's-it? Underwrites, is that the word?"

"I guess."

"Underwrites her research."

"Research?"

"Oh, yeah. Miz Riddle's a doctor."

"Medical doctor."

"Yes, but not the kind that hangs out a shingle. She's some kind of scientific genius."

"So she's doing medical research out there?"

"I guess." She shook her head. "Pity about Bill. Such a nice fella."

"Had he been drinking heavy?"

"Bill? Naw. Oh, he liked a drink. I suppose he shut his share of bars down on a Saturday night, but he wasn't no alcoholic. Not like that other guy."

"What other guy?"

Her expression turned distant. "Funny."

"What's funny? *What* other guy?"

"Not funny ha ha. Funny weird. That other guy, don't remember his name, just some tramp who come through, he was a crip, too."

"A crip?"

"Yeah. He had one arm. Guess he lost his in the war, too. He was working out at the Riddle mansion, as a handyman—one-handed handyman. That guy, he really was a drunk."

"What became of him?"

"That's what's funny weird. Three, four months ago, he wound up like Bill. They found him in the gutter on Main Street, all bunged up, deader than a bad battery. Hit and run victim—just like Bill."

The wrought-iron gate in the gray-brick wall stood open and I tooled the heap up a winding red-brick drive across a gentle treeless slope where the sprawling gabled tan-brick gothic mansion crouched like a lion about to pounce. The golf-course of a lawn had its own rough behind the house, a virtual forest preserve that seemed at once to shelter and encroach upon the stark lines of the house.

Steps led to an open cement pedestal of a porch with a massive slab of a wooden door where I had a choice between an ornate iron knocker and a simple doorbell. I rang the bell.

I stood there listening to birds chirping and enjoying the cool breeze that seemed to whisper rain was on its way, despite the golden sunshine reflecting off the lawn. I rang the bell again.

I was about to go around back, to see if there was another door I could try, when that massive slab of wood creaked open like the start of the "Inner Sanctum" radio program; the three-hundred-and-fifty pound apparition who stood suddenly before me would have been at home on a spook show, himself.

He was six four, easy, towering over my six-one; he wore the black uniform of a chauffeur, but no cap, his tie a loose black string thing. He looked like an upended Buick with a person painted on it. His head was the shape of a grape and just as hairless, though considerably larger; he had no eyebrows either, wide, bugling eyes, a lump of a nose and an open mouth.

"*Unnggh,*" he said.

"I'd like to see Miss Riddle," I said.

"*Unnggh,*" he said.

"It's about Bill Reynolds. I represent his family. I'm here to ask some questions."

His brow furrowed in something approaching thought.

Then he slammed the door in my face.

Normally, I don't put up with crap like that. I'd been polite. He'd been rude. Kicking the door in, and his teeth, seemed called for. Only this boy was a walking side of beef that gave even Mike Hammer pause.

And I was, in fact, pausing, wondering whether to ring the bell again, go around back, or just climb in my heap and drive the hell away, when the door opened again and the human Buick was replaced by a human goddess.

She was tall, standing eye to eye with me, and though she wore a loose-fitting white lab jacket that hung low over a simple black dress, nylons and flat shoes, those mountain-road curves Bill had mentioned were not easily hidden. Her dark blonde hair was tied back, and severe black-frame glasses rode the perfect little nose; she wore almost no make-up, perhaps just a hint of lipstick, or was that the natural color of those full lips? Whatever effort she'd made to conceal her beauty behind a mask of scientific sterility was futile: the big green eyes, the long lashes, the high cheekbones, the creamy complexion, that full-high-breasted, wasp-waisted, long-limbed figure, all conspired to make her as stunning a female creature as God had ever created.

"I'm sorry," she said, in a silky contralto. "This is a private residence and a research center. We see no one without an appointment."

"The gate was open."

"We're expecting the delivery of certain supplies this evening," she said, "and I leave the gate standing open on such occasions. You see, I'm short-handed. But why am I boring you with this? Good afternoon . . ."

And the door began to close.

I held it open with the flat of my hand. "My name is Michael Hammer."

The green eyes narrowed. "The detective?"

I grinned. "You must get the New York papers up here."

"We do. Hopeful isn't the end of the world."

"It was for Bill Reynolds."

Her expression softened, and she cracked the door open, wider. "Poor Bill. Were you a friend?"

"Yes."

"So you've come to ask about his death."

"That's right." I shrugged. "I'm a detective."

"Of course," she said, opening the door. "And you're looking into the circumstances. A natural way for you to deal with such a loss . . ."

She gestured for me to enter, and I followed her through a high-ceilinged entryway. The hairless ape appeared like an apparition and took my trenchcoat; I kept my porkpie hat, but took it off, out of deference to my hostess.

In front of me, a staircase led to a landing, then to a second floor; gilt-framed family portraits lined the way. On one side of us was a library with more leather in bindings and chairs than your average cattle herd; on the other was a formal sitting room where elegant furnishings that had been around long enough to become antiques were overseen by a glittering chandelier.

She led me to a rear room and it was as if, startlingly, we'd entered a penthouse apartment—the paintings on the wall were abstract and modern, and the furnishings were, too, with a television/hi-fi console setup and a zebra wet bar with matching stools; but the room was original with the house, or at least the fireplace and mantle indicated as much. Over the fireplace was the only artwork in the room that wasn't abstract: a full-length portrait of my hostess in a low-cut evening gown, a painting that was impossibly lovely with no exaggeration on the part of the artist.

She slipped out of her lab coat, tossing it on a boomerang of a canvas chair, revealing a short-sleeve white blouse providing an understated envelope for an overstated bosom. Undoing her hair, she allowed its length to shimmer to her shoulders. The severe black-framed glasses, however, she left in place.

Her walk was as liquid as mercury in a vial as she got behind the bar and poured herself a martini. "Fix you a drink?"

"Got any beer back there?"

"Light or dark?"

"Dark."

We sat on a metal-legged couch that shouldn't have been comfortable but was; she was sipping a martini, her dark nyloned legs crossed, displaying well-developed calves. For a scientist, she made a hell of a specimen.

I sipped my beer—it was a bottle of German imported stuff, a little bitter for my taste, but very cold.

"That's an interesting butler you got," I said.

"I have to apologize for Bolo," she said, stirring the cocktail with her speared olive. "His tongue was cut out by natives in the Amazon. My father was on an exploratory trip, somehow incurred the wrath of the natives, and Bolo interceded on his behalf. By offering himself, in the native custom, Bolo bought my father's life—but paid with his tongue."

With a kiss-like bite, she plucked the olive from its spear and chewed.

"He doesn't look much like a South American native," I said.

"He isn't. He was a Swedish missionary. My father never told me Bolo's real name . . . but that was what the natives called him."

"And I don't suppose Bolo's told you, either."

"No. But he can communicate. He can write. In English.

His mental capacity seems somewhat diminished, but he understands what's said to him."

"Very kind of you to keep somebody like that around."

"Like what?"

I shrugged. "Handicapped."

"Mr. Hammer . . ."

"Make it Mike—and I'll call you Victoria. Or do you prefer Vicki?"

"How do you know I don't prefer 'Doctor'?"

"Hey, it's okay with me. I played doctor before."

"Are you flirting with me, Mike?"

"I might be."

"Or you might be trying to get me to let my guard down."

"Why—is it up?"

She glanced at my lap. "You tell me."

Now I crossed *my* legs. "Where's your research lab?"

"In back."

"Sorry if I'm interrupting. . . ."

"No. I'm due for a break. I'd like to help you. You see, I thought a lot of Bill. He worked hard. He may not have been the brightest guy around, but he made up for it with enthusiasm and energy. Some people let physical limitations get in their way. Not Bill."

"You must have a thing for taking in strays."

"What do you mean?"

"Well . . . like Bolo. Like Bill. I understand you took in another handicapped veteran, not so long ago."

"That's right. George Wilson." She shook her head sadly. "Such a shame. He was a hard worker, too—"

"He died the same way as Bill."

"I know."

"Doesn't that strike you as . . . a little odd? Overly coincidental?"

"Mike, George was a heavy drinker, and Bill was known to tie one on, himself. It may be coincidental, but I'm sure they aren't the first barroom patrons to wobble into the street after closing and get hit by a car."

"Nobody saw either one of them get hit by a car."

"Middle of the night. These things happen."

"Not twice."

The green eyes narrowed with interest and concern. "What do *you* think happened, Mike?"

"I have no idea—yet. But I'll say this—everybody seemed to like Bill. I talked to a lot of people today, and nobody, except maybe the police chief, had an unkind word to say about Bill. So I'm inclined to think the common factors between Bill and this George Wilson hold the answer. You're one of those common factors."

"But surely not the only one."

"Hardly. They were both war veterans, down on their luck."

"No shortage of those."

"And they were both handicapped."

She nodded, apparently considering these facts, scientist that she was. "Are you staying in Hopeful tonight?"

"No. I got a court appearance in the city tomorrow. I'll be back on the weekend. Poke around some more."

She put a hand on my thigh. "If I think of anything, how can I find you?"

I patted the hand, removed it, stood. "Keep your gate open," I said, putting on my porkpie, "and I'll find you."

She licked her lips; they glistened. "I'll make sure I leave my gate wide open, on Saturday."

I'd gone back into Hopeful, to talk to the night shift at the diner, got nowhere and headed home in the downpour, pissed off at how little I'd learned. Now, with my car in the ditch, and rain lashing down relentlessly, I found myself back at the Riddle mansion well before Saturday. The gate was still open, though—she must not have received that delivery of supplies she'd talked about, yet.

Splashing through puddles on the winding drive, I kept my trenchcoat collars snugged around me as I headed toward the towering brick house. In the daytime, the mansion had seemed striking, a bit unusual; on this black night, illuminated momentarily in occasional flashes of lightning, its gothic angles were eerily abstract, the planes of the building a stark ghostly white.

This time I used the knocker, hammering with it. It wasn't all that late—maybe nine o'clock or a little after. But it felt like midnight and instinctively I felt the need to wake the dead.

Bolo answered the door. The lights in the entryway were out and he was just a big black blot, distinguishable only by that upended Buick shape of his; then the world turned white, him along with it, and when the thunder caught up with the lightning, I damn near jumped.

"Tell your mistress Mr. Hammer's back," I said. "My car's in a ditch and I need—"

That's when the s.o.b. slammed the door in my face. Second time today. A red heat of anger started to rise up around my collar but it wasn't drying me off, even if the shelter of the awning over the slab of porch was keeping me from getting wetter. Only I wasn't sure a human being could be any wetter than this.

When the door opened again, it was Victoria. She wore a

red silk robe, belted tight around her tiny waist. The sheen of the robe and the folds of the silk conspired with her curves to create a dizzying display of pulchritude.

"Mr. Hammer . . . Mike! Come in, come in."

I did. The light in the entryway was on now, and Bolo was there again, taking my drenched hat and coat. I quickly explained to her what had happened.

"With this storm," she said, "and the bridge out, you'll need to stay the night."

"Love to," I said. Mother Hammer didn't raise any fools.

"But you'll have to get out of those wet things," she said. "I think I have an old nightshirt of my father's . . ."

She took me back to that modern sitting room and I was soon in her Pop's nightshirt, swathed in blankets as I sat before the fireplace's glow, its magical flickering soothingly restful, and making her portrait above the fire seem alive, smiling seductively, the bosom in the low-cut gown heaving with passion. Shaking my head, wondering if I'd completely lost my sanity, I tucked my .45 in its speed rig behind a pillow—hardware like that can be distressing to the gentle sensibilities of some females.

When she cracked the door to ask if I was decent, I said, "That's one thing I've never been accused of, but come on in."

Then she was sitting next to me, the red silk gown playing delightful reflective games with the firelight.

"Can I tell you something terrible?" she asked, like a child with an awful secret.

"I hope you will."

"I'm glad your car went in the ditch."

"And here I thought you liked me."

"I do," she said, and she edged closer. "That's why I'm glad."

She seemed to want me to kiss her, so I did, and it was a long, deep kiss, hotter than the fire, wetter than the night, and then my hands were on top of the smoothness of the silk gown. And then they were on the smoothness underneath it. . . .

Later, when she offered me a guest bedroom upstairs, I declined.

"This is fine," I said, as she made herself a drink behind the bar, and got me another German beer. "I'll just couch it. Anyway, I like the fire."

She handed me the bottle of beer, its cold wetness in my palm contrasting with the warmth of the room, and the moment. Sitting next to me, close to me, she sipped her drink.

"First thing tomorrow," she said, "we'll call into town for a tow truck, and get your car pulled out of that ditch."

"No hurry."

"Don't you have a court appearance tomorrow?"

"Acts of God are a good excuse," I said, and rested the beer on an amoeba-shaped coffee table nearby, then leaned in and kissed her again. Just a friendly peck.

"Aren't you thirsty?" she asked, nodding toward the beer.

Why was she so eager for me to drink that brew?

I said, "Dry as a bone," and reached for the bottle, lifted it to my lips, and seemed to take a drink.

Seemed to.

Now she gave me a friendly kiss, said, "See you at breakfast," and rose, sashaying out as she cinched the silk robe back up. If you could bottle that walk, you'd really have something worth researching.

Alone, I sniffed the beer. My unscientific brain couldn't detect anything, but I knew damn well it contained a mickey. She wanted me to sleep through this night. I didn't know why, but something was going to happen here that a houseguest like me—even one who'd been lulled into a false sense of security by a very giving hostess—shouldn't see.

So I poured the bottle of beer down the drain and quickly went to the couch and got myself under the blankets and pretended to be asleep.

But I couldn't have been more alert if I'd been in a foxhole on the front line. My eyes only seemed shut; they were slitted open and saw her when she peeked in to see if I was sleeping. I even saw her mouth and eyes tighten in smug satisfaction before the door closed, followed by the click of me being locked in. . . .

The rain was still sheeting down when, wearing only her daddy's nightshirt, I went out a window and, .45 in hand, found my way to the back of the building where a new section had been added on, institutional-looking brick with no windows at all. The thin cotton cloth of the nightshirt was a transparent second skin by the time I found my way around the building and discovered an open double garage, also back behind, following an extension of the original driveway. The garage doors stood open and a single vehicle—a panel truck bearing the Hopeful Police Department insignia—was within, dripping with water, as if it were sweating.

Cautiously, I slipped inside, grateful to be out of the rain. Along the walls of the garage were various boxes and crates with medical supply house markings. I could hear approaching footsteps and ducked behind a stack of crates.

Peeking out, I could see Chief Dolbert, in a rain slicker and matching hat, leading the way for Bolo, still in his chauffeur-type uniform. Dolbert opened up the side of the van and Bolo leaned in.

And when Bolo leaned back out, he had his arms filled with a person, a woman in fact, a naked one; then Bolo walked away from the panel truck, toward the door back into the building, held open for him by the thoughtful police chief. It was as if Bolo were carrying a bride across the threshold.

Only this bride was dead.

For ten minutes I watched as Bolo made trips from the building to the panel truck, where with the chief's assistance he conveyed naked dead bodies into the house. My mind was reeling with the unadorned horror of it. I was shivering and not just from the water-soaked nightshirt I was in. Somehow, being in that nightshirt, naked under it, made me feel a kinship to these poor dead bastards, many of them desiccated-looking souls, with unkempt hair and bony ill-fed bodies, and finally it came to me.

I knew who these poor dead wretches were. And I knew why, at least roughly why, Chief Dolbert was delivering them.

When at last the doors on the panel truck were shut, the chief and Bolo headed back into the building. That pleased me—I was afraid the chief would take off into the rainy, thunderous night, and I didn't want him to.

I wanted him around.

Not long after they had disappeared into the building, I went in after them.

And into Hell.

It was a blindingly well-illuminated Hell, a white and silver Hell, resembling a hospital operating room but much larger, a Hell dominated by the silver of surgical instruments, a Hell where the walls were lined with knobs and dials and meters and gizmos, a Hell dominated by naked corpses on metal autopsy-type tables, their empty eyes staring at the bright overhead lighting.

And the sensual satan who ruled over this Hell, Victoria Riddle, who was back in her lab coat now, hair tucked in a bun, was filling the open palm of Chief Dolbert with greenbacks.

But where was Bolo?

I glanced behind me, and there he was, tucked behind the door, standing like a cigar store Indian awaiting his mistress' next command, only she didn't have to give this command: Bolo knew enough to reach out for this intruder, his hands clawed, his eyes bulging to where the whites showed all around, his mouth open in a soundless snarl.

"Stop!" I told the looming figure, as he threw his shadow over me like a blue blanket.

But he didn't stop.

And when I blew the top of his bald head off, splashing the white wall behind him with the colors of the inside of his head, red and gray and white, making another abstract painting only without a frame, that didn't stop him either, didn't stop him from falling on top of me, and by the time I had pushed his massive dead weight off of me, his fat corpse emptying ooze out the top of his bald blown-off skull, I had another fat bastard to deal with, a *live* one: the chief of the Hopeful police department, his revolver pointed down at me.

"Drop it," he said.

He should have just shot me, because I took advantage of his taking time to say that and shot him, in the head, and the gun in his hand was useless now, since his brain could no longer send it signals, and he toppled back on top of one of the corpses, sharing its silver tray, staring up at the ceiling, the red hole in his forehead like an extra expressionless eye.

"You fool," she said, the lovely face lengthening into a contorted ugly mask, green eyes wild behind the glasses.

"I decided I wasn't thirsty after all," I said, as I weaved my way between the corpses on their metal slabs.

"You don't understand! This is serious research! This will benefit *humanity* . . ."

"I understand you were paying the chief for fresh cadavers," I said. "With him in charge of the state's potter's field, you had no shortage of dead guinea pigs. But what I *don't* understand is, why kill Bill, and George Wilson, when you had access to all these riches?"

And I gestured to the deceased indigents around us.

Her face eased back into beauty; her scientific mind had told her, apparently, that her best bet now was to try to reason with me. Calmly. Coolly.

I was close enough to her to kiss her, only I didn't feel much like kissing her and, anyway, the .45 I was aiming at her belly would have been in the way of an embrace.

"George Wilson tried to blackmail me," she said. "Bill . . . Bill just wouldn't cooperate. He said he was going to the authorities."

"About your ghoulish arrangement with the chief, you mean?"

She nodded. Then earnestness coated her voice: "Mike, I was only trying to *help* Bill, and George—*and* mankind. Don't you see? I wanted to make them *whole* again!"

"Oh my God," I said, getting it. "Bill was a *live* guinea pig, wasn't he? Wilson, too . . ."

"That's not how I'd express it, exactly, but yes . . ."

"You wanted to make them living Frankenstein monsters . . . you wanted to sew the limbs of the dead on 'em . . ."

Her eyes lighted up with enthusiasm, and hope. And madness. "Yes! *Yes!* I learned in South America of Voodoo techniques that reanimated the dead into so-called 'zombies.' The scientific community was sure to reject such 'mumbo jumbo' and deny the world this wonder, and I have been forced to seek the truth with my mixture of the so-called supernatural and renegade science. With the correct tissue matches, and my own research into electro-chemical transplant techniques . . ."

That was when the lights went out.

God's electricity had killed man's electricity, and the cannon roar aftermath of the thunderbolt wasn't enough to hide the sound of her scurrying in the dark amongst the trays of the dead, trying to escape, heading for that door onto the garage.

I went after her, but she had knowledge of the layout of the place and I didn't, I kept bumping into bodies, and then she screamed.

Just for a split second.

A hard *whump* had interrupted the scream, and before I even had time to wonder what the hell had happened, the lights came back on, and there she was.

On her back, on the floor, her head resting against the metal underbar of one of the dead-body trays, only resting wasn't really the word, since she'd hit hard enough to crack open her skull and a widening puddle of red was forming below her head as she too stared up at the ceiling with wide-open eyes, just another corpse in a roomful of corpses. Bolo's dead body, where I'd pushed his dead weight off of me, was—as was fitting—at his mistress' feet.

I had to smile.

Bolo may not have had many brains in that chrome dome of his, but he'd had enough to slip her up.

SO LONG, CHIEF

The old man was dying, but there was nobody to see him off. In a few more days he'd get the royal farewell, a eulogy by the police chaplain, a cavalcade of motorcycle troops, and a final salute from the fresh young faces to whom he was nothing but a fading legend. He was the last of the old breed who had outlived his friends and his usefulness and he was all alone on his final assignment.

The nurse said, "Not too long, please."

She was a cute brunette in her twenties, well worth flirting with, but I wasn't in the mood.

I asked, "Pretty bad?"

Her answer was only slightly evasive: "He's almost ninety, tires easily. Are you family?"

"No," I said. "He doesn't have any family."

She gave me a little smile and nodded. "I see. Just don't excite him."

I could have told her that there wasn't much that could ever excite him after the life he'd lived.

But I just said my thanks and went into the sterile little hospital room with the green walls and the automated bed that seemed to hold him like a waiter balancing a tray. Hard to believe that once he would have dominated a room of any size like the Colossus of Rhodes. Now he was just a textured form under the sheet.

But the unmistakable quality was there, a strange force as alive as ever, hovering like a protective screen around his withered face.

I walked to the bed, looked down at him and said, "Hello, Chief."

He didn't open his eyes. He simply let the tone of my voice go through a mental computer check and when it didn't register, he said, "You one of the new ones?"

"Not really."

When he turned his head he let his eyes slide open and the old tiger was still in there. For a good five seconds he was riffling through the cerebral filing cabinet before he satisfied himself that I was clean . . . at least up to a point.

"I don't know you," he stated in a curiously noncommital voice.

"No reason why you should. It's been a long time, Chief. Forty-some years."

The voice still had strength, shrouded though it was in a growly rasp. "You'd have been a little kid then."

"Uh-huh. About eleven. A wise-ass young punk in a lousy neighborhood who was prepping himself for all that beautiful mob action he saw around him . . . the rolls of dough, the fancy cars, a string of lovely broads, just the way Gino Madoni had it."

The tiger stirred behind the eyes. It crouched, the lips curling back over huge shiny white fangs.

"I shot Madoni myself," the Chief said.

"Yeah you did. You were a fresh-faced boyo who just made detective wading into something way the hell over his head."

". . . and you were . . . ?"

"I was the little kid you rapped the living shit out of, the twerp who carried policy slips around in his school bag."

He was remembering now, and letting the pieces fall into a knowable pattern. *The tiger's tail twitched.* "The little kid never forgot, did he?"

I grinned at him. "Nope. It was a lesson that stuck with him."

Maybe it was my grin that did it, but the tiger suddenly hesitated, poised to pounce but curious.

I said, "That punk kid never forgot a lot of things. Like how Gino tore that girl up in that cellar and then broke old man Kravitch's arm for him. Or how Gino was always talking about how some day he was gonna kill himself a cop, only when one finally came in after him, for shooting a guard in a hold-up, Gino went all to pieces. Grabbed that kid and held him in front of him, thinking the cop wouldn't shoot with the kid as a shield, but forgetting the cop was a damn good shot who could take him out, kid or no kid. That cop, that young detective, put a slug in Gino's head and that kid got splashed with the kind of memory you don't forget."

". . . Is that what you came here to say?"

"In part, Chief. There's something else, too."

"Say it then."

"I just came to say so long."

The tiger, as wary as age and experience could make it, was not quite sure what it was looking at. The fangs should have been yellowed and broken, but they weren't. They were still shiny white.

For some reason, this old stick of a man felt he could still handle me, if need be.

His voice was like rough steel scraping rougher steel. "Why the visit, after half a lifetime?"

"Because that kid remembered his lesson and what the detective said."

"What did the detective say?"

"Oh, nothing flowery. Just, 'Don't wind up like that dead dago, laddie-buck.' He could've grabbed that kid and shook him till his teeth rattled, shoving fear up the kid's ass just for the fun of it."

"But he didn't."

I shook my head.

"So. Did the kid get the point?"

I shrugged. "Well, he didn't turn out to be another Gino Madoni."

"Good to hear. How *did* he turn out?"

"He went to the other side, and now he's here to say thanks and so long to the guy who put him there."

"And . . . that's all?"

I shrugged again. "Why else? I'm glad I made it up here in time. We were two eras, Chief, that didn't overlap that much. But I owe you. Funny, considering you retired before I even got on the job."

"You were on the PD, son?"

"Briefly. Private now. For a long time. An old friend told me your situation, and where you were."

"What old friend?"

"Captain Pat Chambers."

Gently, the tiger withdrew, no longer hungry. "You're pretty big," the Chief said. "You tough?"

"I manage."

"Married?"

"No."

With the tiger out of them, the eyes were those of an old fighter in his last round, still circling an adversary he knew he couldn't beat, but wanting to get in one last lick anyway, before the bell rang.

"You appreciate that favor I did you?" He spoke the words as though he were tasting them.

"I'm here," I reminded him.

His left hand came out from under the sheet and he pointed toward the closet across the room. "There's a box in there. Get it."

I could feel something funny happening, some odd charge flickering from the finger to the closet and back to me again. It was something I didn't particularly like because it wasn't new to me at all. It made my belly go tight and the skin crawl across my shoulders, but the finger was pointing and I went and got the old metal box and put it on the bed beside him. His fingers shook with age and fatigue as he turned the small combination dial to its three digits, then lifted the lid.

In the dim light, I could see the papers and knew what they were: select items from a thirty-five year span of active duty, including the citation ribbons and the worn leather wallet that held the badge of the highest rank in the department.

He was watching my face and I saw a faint smile move his lips. Then he reached in the box, felt in a corner and brought out a key. He looked at it a few seconds, then handed it to me. "This is for you."

"What's it open?"

"That's for you to find out," he said. He wasn't smiling now. "A lot of people are going to be looking for that key. I thought that was what you came here for."

"I only came to say so long, Chief."

"Yeah. I know. That's why I gave it to you. Now get the hell out of here. I'm tired."

"Sure, Chief." But I stood there for a moment, key in my fist, watching with the pride of knowing him, and was almost about to ask the question when he answered me first.

"They couldn't have taken it from me," he said.

Then he took his right hand out from under the covers, let me look at his old .38 Police Positive before he handed it to me and wrapped his fingers around mine as they held the weapon. "A good piece, son. Take care of it."

I checked the load, closed the cylinder and stuck it in my belt. The last time I had seen that gun was when it tore the head off a guy who was risking getting me killed to save his own hide. I started to tell the old boy thanks, but his eyes were closed and his hand slipped away from mine. The rhythm of his breathing was barely perceptible under the sheet.

Trying to be quiet, I walked to the door, but before I got there, he said, "I didn't get your name."

"Mike," I told him. "Mike Hammer."

". . . I should have known. You . . . made your name after I retired."

"I did. I never came around because, well . . ."

"You thought I might not approve of your tactics."

"Yeah."

His smile was a crease among the many creases in the gaunt face. "Guess again."

I could hear him chuckling behind me as I closed the door.

The cute nurse at her counter said, "Does he need anything?"

"No. Not now."

"He was a big man in this city, in his day, wasn't he?"

"A great man. Great old guy."

It was quiet in a ward that wasn't the kind that attracted too many visitors. The smell of age and death made this pretty brunette nurse so full of life a vague insult, a shout of youth in a silence that came from being forgotten and left alone in a still place, alone until the priest came around, anyway.

I asked, "Anybody ever come to see him?"

"One old man in a wheelchair," she said.

"Any idea who he was?"

"A retired policeman from the nursing home where the patient lived. A male attendant brought him around."

"What nursing home?"

"Long Island Care Center."

"Nobody else?"

"Like you said—he had no family."

"Yes he has."

"Oh?" Her psychological training was showing in the frown under her cap. Then her business administration side took over and she yanked a drawer open to check her files.

I saved her the trouble.

"I meant me," I told her.

Her smile remained very businesslike and professional. If I were dying in a hospital ward, and she smiled at me any way at all, I'd bust out crying.

She said, "Oh, I'm sorry. Are you his son?"

For fun I gave her a big tiger grin like the Chief used to have.

"No, doll," I said. "Just a great big fucking ghost out of the distant past."

She blinked long lashes at me. "May I . . . may I . . . have your name?"

"Sure, honey. Mike. Mike Hammer."

She frowned. "I've heard that name before."

"Well, that'll make me easier to remember, in case I didn't make an impression."

I went downstairs and got in my car.

Ten minutes later, somebody slipped into the Chief's room and stuck a knife between his ribs, robbing him of the hours or maybe minutes he had left.

But at least they didn't get the key.

"All this heat's unnecessary, Pat," I said to the Captain of Homicide who was sucking himself back in the shadows of his office while the D.A. was riding me. "Tell this big shot I just got back from Florida, and I already have a tan."

I'd made an impression on that cute nurse, all right. She'd remembered my name just fine, as her murdered patient's last visitor, when the cops had asked.

I was sitting in a hard chair in Pat's office, ankle on a knee, with my back to his desk where I'd tossed my hat. I gave the D.A. a tight-lipped smile that meant screw the politicians and turned back to Inspector Milroy, who had already read me my rights and was trying like hell to get a confession out of me.

I said, "Either charge me and book me, or let me go."

The D.A. frowned. It gave his blankly handsome face a little character, at least. "Mr. Hammer. . . ."

"Talk to my lawyer."

He shook his head, threw up his hands and stormed out, shutting the door behind him so hard it gave the window glass the shakes. But Milroy stayed at it. We'd tangled asses many times over the years, and which of us hated the other more was up for grabs. He was in his sixties but still dangerous, blond hair mingled white now, husky and florid, with a scar across his forehead from an automobile crash. When his face got red, it stood out like a vertical lightning bolt. Like now.

"There was a metal box in that room," Milroy said. "It was open, and the contents scattered about. Did you *take* something, Hammer?"

"What, after I killed him you mean? Yeah, there was a Cadillac in there. I drove it down the hall. Didn't the nurse tell you?"

He bared teeth the color of sweet corn, but there wasn't anything sweet about the two big fists he raised to his chest, hunching as he moved forward, lumbering closer.

"Please," I said. "Please do it. I been waiting years for this."

Pat was behind him then, his hands latched onto the big cop's shoulders, holding him back, speaking softly, gently, into his ear: "I know what the Chief meant to you. But you can't do it this way, Inspector. You can't throw thirty years away."

When Milroy turned toward Pat, they were close enough to kiss, only Milroy was sputtering, spitting. "Why, if I take this monkey apart, you'll testify on *his* behalf? Are you two *really* that tight, Chambers?"

"Yes," Pat said.

Milroy shuddered, shaking his arms till his fists turned into fingers. He seemed to relax, but his face was still bunched up. He straightened his tie. "Shit," he said.

"Anyway," Pat said, "you wouldn't take him apart. He's twenty years younger and fifty pounds lighter, Inspector, and I'd be trading this problem for a new one."

"Yeah?"

"Yeah. Mike would kill you, and I'd be very unpopular around here when I went on the record saying it was self-defense."

I was rocking back in a hard chair, grinning. "I can step outside, if you girls want to be alone."

"Some day, Hammer," Milroy said. "Some day."

"Better rush it. You're retiring soon, right? Make sure I get an invite to the gold watch party."

The inspector pushed Pat aside, hard enough that the Homicide Captain damn near lost his balance, and the door slammed again, giving that glass its second stress test in five minutes.

Pat sighed. Now it was his turn to straighten his tie. "You are a hobby I wish I didn't have, Mike."

"Interesting new interrogation technique. The cops yell at each other. Maybe you should take it up a notch. Rough each other up some."

"Not funny, Mike. Not funny." Pat got behind his desk and fired up a Lucky. He didn't offer me one—he knew I'd quit. So had he—a dozen times. "Anything you want to tell me that you didn't want the D.A. and my superior to know?"

"If that guy's your 'superior,' Liberace's a better ivory tickler than Van Cliburn."

"Liberace's more popular. Spill, Mike. What are you holding back?"

Nothing much—just a little metal key.

"Not a damn thing, Pat. Would I hold out on you?"

"You wouldn't give me the time of day if my watch was broken."

"Now that's just unkind. So Milroy is taking this personally, huh? He was that close to the Chief?"

Pat nodded. "Working out of the Chief's office till the old boy retired. What was the Chief to you, Mike? He retired before you made your rep. Did he even know who you were?"

"He didn't recognize the face, but the name he knew." I shrugged. "When I was a kid, and he wasn't the Chief yet, he did me a favor."

"So are you going on the warpath like Milroy? Will I have two Mike Hammers to deal with this time around?"

"Naw. But I am curious about why anybody on his death bed is worth a knife in the ribs."

"I don't have an answer yet."

"Yeah, and that Milroy character will get the answer right after you find Judge Crater. Maybe I *should* take an interest."

"No, Mike . . . no. . . ."

I got to my feet. "Who would want to kill the Chief at this late date, Pat? What did he ever do in any of his yesterdays to buy what he got today?"

Pat sighed blue smoke. "He was a crusader, the Chief. Before you came along with your one-man war on the Evello outfit, he was the only guy who ever stood up against the mobsters. Put a shitload of 'em away. And before the Knapp Commission, he was the only official in the city to make a real effort at cleaning up the department. He fired and jailed dozens of bent cops, back before the war."

"So he made enemies." I slapped my hat on. "Enemies enough to kill him?"

"Oh yeah."

I was almost out the door when I said, "What took them so long?"

And I took it easy on the glass, shutting it nice and gentle on the puzzled puss of Captain Patrick Chambers.

In the old Hackard Building, in the outer office of the door labeled MICHAEL HAMMER INVESTIGATIONS, my secretary Velda sat behind her desk studying the little key like it unlocked the secrets of life. In this case, the secret of a death was more likely.

She's a big girl, my Velda, all curves and raven-wing hair in a pageboy that went out of style a long time ago, and to hell with style. She wore a simple pale pink blouse and a short navy skirt that with her in it put to shame anything Frederick's of Hollywood ever came up with. And she's my secretary like Watson is Holmes' family practitioner—she has a PI license and packs a flat little automatic in her purse between her compact and her lipstick.

"Not a safe deposit box," she said, turning it in tapering fingers with blood-red nails. "No numbers."

"It's old," I said. "Something's been locked away for a long time. So it's not a bus station locker. They check those daily."

"Did he maintain a membership at the police gym? Those lockers would be old enough."

"Vel, he was eighty-nine. I don't think he played intramural basketball anymore."

"Maybe it's to another metal box. Buried or hidden somewhere."

"Maybe."

She hefted it in her palm, up and down, up and down. "A little big to unlock a desk drawer. A little small to unlock a shed."

"Doesn't look like a padlock key."

"No, or a file cabinet key, either. To me, it's a locker key, but where? Boat club maybe?"

"You got me. He's been living at a nursing home. Long Island Care Center. We should go out there."

Velda nodded and got the Long Island book out of a drawer.

I stood and rested an ass cheek on the edge of her desk. She had the book open and was about to dial when she asked, "But *what* did the Chief have locked away? Money?"

"Naw. He had something on somebody."

She frowned. "Evidence? Of a crime? Would he withhold that? You said he was a straight arrow."

"Straight arrows have been known to make deals with the devil."

"You're mixing your metaphors, Mike."

"Maybe so, but the Chief made a lot of enemies, like Pat said. Why did one of 'em wait so long to take revenge? Whoever it was didn't cheat the Grim Reaper out of much."

She nodded, started to dial, then hung up abruptly, her dark eyes flaring. "Mike, that's it."

"What is?"

"It's evidence. He *did* have something on somebody. A long time ago the Chief told somebody that if anything ever happened to him, this evidence would come out."

I slipped off the desk. "And for years and years that evidence . . . a gun, a ledger book, a signed statement . . . was safely tucked away where it could do no harm."

She shook a lecturing finger at me. "But then the Chief was marked for death, not by some hitman, but by time and tide."

I was nodding. "And on his death bed, the Chief would have been fine with that evidence finally catching up with whatever devil he'd made a deal with."

She was shaking her head, the dark locks bouncing off her shoulders. "But what kind of deal would that be? What kind of crime would a straight shooter like the Chief conceal? Maybe you need to face it, Mike. Maybe he wasn't the god you thought he was. Maybe he had feet of clay like the rest of us."

"Clay is what I'll have on the bottom of my shoes," I said, "when I walk over the grave of the bastard who knifed him."

"I can't top that one," Velda said with a smirk, and finally dialed that goddamn phone.

Leaving the steel-stone-and-glass tombstones of Manhattan behind, we had a pleasant drive in light traffic out to Long Island. The spring afternoon was so nice that when I spoke to retired Police Sergeant Carl Spooner, he and I sat outside on a cement patio, facing bushes and trees whose leaves shimmered with sunshine. I was in a kind of lawn chair, and the old sarge was in a wheelchair.

We knew each other just a little. He'd been the desk sergeant for a while at the precinct house Pat worked out of maybe twenty years ago. A nod and a wave kind of friendship, not enough to justify a visit to a nursing home in the sticks.

"I bet this is about the Chief," the Sarge said.

He had been big once, but he'd shrunk, swimming in a white shirt and tan slacks, his big shoulders now just massive hunched bookends for a sunken chest. His cheeks were sunken, too, and his nose was like an Indian arrowhead stuck on there. His blue eyes were rheumy but still sharp.

"You should've gone for detective," I said.

"Naw, not me. I was a born desk sergeant. It's an art, you know. You got to deal with all kinds. Mostly not the cream of the crop, if you get my drift. You know what we used to say? We used to say, it ain't the heat, it's the humanity."

"Yeah, but not a bad gig. Get to rule the roost."

"Got that right. Where'd that big doll of yours go? The one that reminds me what it was I used to like about women. I saw her come in with you."

"She's talking to your head administrator."

"About the Chief?"

"About the Chief. You and I have something in common, Sarge."

"What would that be?"

"We were the last two people to see him alive."

Not counting his killer.

"Is that right?" he said.

I nodded toward the wheelchair. "You went to a lot of trouble to visit him."

"They got people here to help out. They got a van they drive you around in for doctor appointments and shit." The big shoulders on the frail body lifted and dropped. "Anyway, the Chief, he was a buddy. You have to say so long to a buddy."

"You two go back a long way?"

"Naw, not at all. Hell, he was the Chief. We never even met when I was on the job. I mean, I saw him on the stage at functions, handing out medals and such. Shook his hand in a receiving line once. It was out here we got to be buds. Two old coppers stuck in stir together." He cackled.

"You got close, these last few years?"

"Damn straight. Look around you, Mike. You'll learn an important lesson."

"What's that?"

"A man can live *too* long. The Chief outlived his two kids and a wife he adored. One of the most important men in the city, reduced to sittin' around jawin' with a lowly desk sergeant."

"Nobody came out to see him?"

"Now and again, a few coppers who served under him. That inspector that worked for him. That captain you used to stop around the precinct house to visit."

"Chambers?"

"Yeah. Pat Chambers! Man, I haven't heard that name in years. You guys were asshole buddies, weren't you?"

"Still are. Anybody else?"

"No. Like I said, he outlived his family. You know, the Chief was retired for over thirty years. He and his wife moved out here somewhere. Besides his family, the only thing he said he missed was playing golf. Him and some other retired department bigwigs used to go to the Oakland Golf Club in Queens. But they're all dead, too."

On the ride back, Velda shared what she'd learned from the nursing home's top administrator.

"There's something that Pat held back from you," Velda said, green countryside gliding by behind her in the passenger window.

"Maybe you better give me a second to get over the shock of that."

"Two big men, not young, maybe in their fifties or even sixties, were seen in the nursing home hallways yesterday. One asked where the Chief's room was, but otherwise they had no contact with staff. They were in suit and tie, and the assumption was they were visitors or were scoping the place out for an elderly parent. The Long Island cops already gathered that info and passed it along to Pat."

"So they searched the Chief's room, came up empty . . . and tried again this morning, at the hospital?"

She nodded. "Where they found his metal box that he'd taken along with him . . . but not his gun and that key."

Now I was nodding. "Only that sheaf of papers representing a career of dedication. Which was worthless to them."

She hadn't learned much else from the administrator. The

Chief had been a resident for eight years. His income had been reduced to his pension and Social Security, and his meager possessions, mostly clothing, had been left to the facility for anybody who could use them. The scraps were all that remained of a great man and a fine life. The Sarge was right—a man could live too long.

Then I filled Velda in on what the old desk sergeant had told me.

"A golf club," she said, dark eyes flashing. "Damn. That could be it. *There's* your locker! Where is the place? Let's go over there."

"We're driving over it. It was knocked down to make room for the expressway."

She frowned. "Mike—that means you might have a key to a locker that doesn't exist anymore."

"Maybe. But the Chief surely knew that Oak View was a victim of progress, and that was fifteen years ago. There's a possibility he and his golfing buddies from the department found another course."

She nodded. "We can only hope. . . . What now?"

"Now I need to get back to the office. I'll drop you at your apartment."

Her frown was deep. "The office? Why? It's not like *you* handle the paperwork."

"Your Mike has his reasons."

"That's what I'm afraid of."

But she didn't push it. She knew I was up to something, but she also knew that if I wanted her in on it, I'd tell her. Still, her lovely dark eyes were on me the rest of the way back.

I stretched out in my shirtsleeves on the black leather couch in my inner office. When I'd got back around dusk, I left the lights off, took the carry-out paper bag to my desk, and sat there making a corned beef sandwich and a cup of coffee disappear.

Soon I was on the couch in the near dark, the city outside the window behind my desk fighting the night with a million lights. I could have shut that out by adjusting the blinds, but I wasn't anxious to go to sleep. Now, on my back with my suit-coat and shoes off, I lay there staring at a ceiling I could barely see with my .45 on the floor next to me.

Was the key to the mystery the key in my pocket? Was the only way to figure out who killed the Chief to find out what that little scrap of ancient metal unlocked?

Were the two men who had searched the Chief's nursing home room looking for that key, or did they even know of its existence? Did they seek instead whatever evidence the Chief had hidden away, for the key to unlock?

One thing I *did* know was why someone had bothered murdering a man who was already inches from death—they needed to silence the Chief while looking for the key or what the key represented. The contents of that metal box had been strewn around, that inspector said, indicating the Chief's only slightly premature death had bought his killer or killers time to toss his hospital room.

Where there had been nothing to find.

Because *I* had that key, didn't I?

But whatever it unlocked seemed out of reach—in an old locker somewhere, at a golf club maybe . . . if it wasn't under tons of concrete. Possibly at some other locker or storage facility—who the hell knew?

That's for you to find out, the Chief had told me.

Which meant Velda and I should be able to track it down.

The Chief had lived a lot of life, and lives could always be sifted through—we did it all the time. Of course, most of the people the Chief had shared that life with were gone.

So we were facing a long investigation both exhaustive and exhausting, with no guarantee we'd come up with a damn thing. But what other option was there?

There was one.

I could camp out here in my office and wait for the answer to walk through my door. That I had been the last to see the Chief alive before his killer—or killers—was no secret. The hospital knew. The cops knew. The press would probably know by now.

I would almost certainly have after-hours visitors.

Despite my best intentions, I did drift off, but nothing deep, nothing with dreams in it, and I sure as hell wasn't dreaming when a click announced somebody picking the lock on my office door.

I reached down for the .45, its cold rough grip comforting in my grasp.

They were talking out there, too muffled for me to make out, but they weren't bothering to whisper. A glance at my wristwatch said it was almost ten o'clock. Nobody in the building at this hour but cleaning staff, their routine an hour away from the eighth floor, anyway.

The couch was against the side wall, so I would have a perfect view of my callers when they came through my inner office door. But they were tossing the outer area first. Bold bastards—another click sent glow crawling under my inner-office door, meaning they had switched the lights on out there. I heard file cabinet and desk drawers opening. Some occasional talk. Not working at making no noise, but not making a racket, either.

I could have waited for them to finish out there, but it just wasn't my way. Who the hell knew what kind of mess they'd make if I didn't put a stop to this? I slipped off the couch, padded over in my socks to the door connecting the inner and outer office.

I opened it, fast.

"Nobody has to die," I said.

Velda's desk was just a few feet forward, and one guy was behind it, with a drawer open. He looked back at me with the expression of an adulterer caught by a cuckold. He was maybe four feet away to my immediate right, his pal across the room at the row of file cabinets to my left, still working on the top drawer, its contents spilled on the floor.

In that split second I knew them—they were old-time thugs, Mafia boys easily twenty years older than me and unlikely soldiers to be sent on any mission. Their suits were baggy and their ties were wide, their clothes as out of date as they were. I hadn't seen them around in years—one's last name was Rossi, the other's first name Salvo, which was the best my brain could come up with on short notice.

They were frozen, almost comically so, Rossi nearby at Velda's desk, half-turned to me, a once handsome guy gone badly to seed, his eyebrows black but his hair gray against dark skin tanned deep brown. Over at the file cabinet, Salvo stood sideways, as pale as his partner was dark, a stringbean with a healthy head of curly black hair, though the pouchy face looking at me had the kind of miles on it that got you replaced if you were a Firestone.

My voice was calm and my gun hand was steady. "There are two chairs over by the wall. Go over there slow and sit. We're gonna talk. I might not even call the cops if you cooperate."

This was much better treatment than they deserved, breaking into my fucking office at ten o'clock at night, but I wanted information, not satisfaction.

Too bad Salvo thought he had the advantage on me. He thought I hadn't noticed he'd set a revolver down on the file cabinet top, and when he went for it, I put one in his head and bloody brain matter glopped onto the far wall. *Goddamnit*, there went the information I wanted, dripping down the plaster.

Ears ringing from the rattling roar of the gunshot, I swung the .45 over toward Rossi, to see if he was smart enough to hold up his hands. But he was going for a rod in a holster under his shoulder, figuring that me killing his partner would give him time. I wondered when he'd last been sent out on a real job, because if he'd been any slower, I could have just slapped the thing out of his hand. Instead, he was just fast enough to get himself killed. The bullet in his forehead shut his life off like a switch and he thudded sideways into Velda's desk, knocking over and shattering her favorite vase.

There would be hell to pay for that.

When he slid down, he accidentally shut the drawer he'd opened, then sat there, legs straight out in front of him, staring into nothing, his right hand still open and reaching for the gun he never even touched.

"Okay, then," I said. "We'll do it your way."

Salvo was similarly situated by the file cabinet, and I got one piece of information out of him, anyway—that black curly hair had shifted, revealing itself as a wig.

I shook my head, holstered the .45, and walked back to Velda's desk, stepping around the bloody array of brains that had showered our new carpet out of the back of Rossi's skull. So much for preventing a mess in the outer office.

I reached for the phone, to call Pat at home.

"Leonardo Rossi," Pat said, "and Salvatore Ferraro."

I was sitting behind my desk, the big rangy Homicide captain in the client chair opposite, while in the outer office his elves were scurrying—a crime lab team, a photographer, and a plainclothes dick, with a couple of uniformed men in the hall. The bodies hadn't been hauled away yet.

"I better call Velda," I said absently. "If she comes in to work tomorrow and finds crime scene tape blocking the way, I'll never hear the end of it."

Pat leaned forward and the gray-blue eyes narrowed. "Don't duck me, buddy. What brought these two long-in-the-tooth goombahs away from the bocce ball court and into your little trap?"

"My what?"

"Come on, Mike. Don't shit a shitter. You were waiting for them. How, *why*, did you know they were coming?"

"Why don't you tell me, Pat?"

Now he leaned back and his smile was cold. "When you visited the Chief, he gave you something. Or you took it. What, Mike? This is an investigation into the homicide of one of this city's great chiefs of police. Don't hold out."

"Like you held out on me?"

"What's that supposed to mean?"

I grunted at him. "You knew two guys had searched the Chief's nursing-home room last night. Guys matching the description of those two overripe lasagne lads, right? And I bet they were seen at the hospital this morning, too. You knew that when you hauled me in for the D.A. and Milroy to roast."

He sighed heavily. Searched his pockets for a deck of smokes and came up with an empty package; he crumpled it up in a crinkly wad and tossed it on my desk. "Why the hell did you have to quit smoking?"

"Your concern for my health is touching, good buddy. Of course, you might have told me a couple of old-time Mafia cannons were on the prowl."

He shook his head. "I didn't know that's who they were till just now. They *do* go way back. Before the war. Vito Madoni's crew, if you can believe that."

I showed no reaction. "Gino Madoni's little brother."

"Yeah. Here's a piece of history I bet you didn't know—the Chief, back when he was a rookie detective, shot Gino and killed his ass. Had him cold on a bank guard killing."

"You don't say. Man, no detail slips past you, does it, Pat?"

"The Chief's also the guy who sent brother Vito to jail, '41 I think it was, and after that, the Madoni family was never a major mob player. If I remember, those two in your reception area are Bonneti boys now, or were until they retired a year or so back."

I rocked in my chair, saying nothing.

Pat said, "What?"

"A couple of Mafia enforcers come out of retirement, to kill the Chief. Suggest anything to you, Pat?"

"Sure it does. Revenge."

"When he's almost dead anyway? No. I think this has more to do with there being no statute of limitations on murder."

"What murder?"

"I don't know. But I got a feeling that over there at Homicide, you may have a few unsolved ones on the books."

113

"Mike, we have thousands of unsolved homicides, dating to Prohibition. You know that."

"Well, I should let you go back home then, and catch some Z's, so you can get to work on them tomorrow, nice and fresh."

"Mike, unless you cop to the Chief giving you some item that those two were looking for, this case will be closed by noon tomorrow. You may not like revenge as a motive, but everybody else will."

"You know what they say—a man's gotta do what a man's gotta do." I got to my feet, yawned. Busy evening. "I'm surprised your buddy Milroy wasn't along for the ride."

Pat shrugged as he stood. "Me, too, actually. I called him and gave him the opportunity. He made me promise to keep him in the loop on this one."

"He passed up an opportunity to bust my balls?"

"Yup. Said I could fill him in tomorrow. Maybe he's mellowing in his old age. . . . Listen, you're free to go, Mike."

"You mean I can leave my own office? Why are you so good to me?"

He just smirked and batted a wave at me, letting me have the exit line.

Only I didn't exit. I sat back down at my desk and thought some more, while some morgue wagon attendants in the outer office were taking out the trash.

The next morning I caught a cab over to One Police Plaza, near City Hall and the Brooklyn Bridge, a thirteen-story pyramidal glass-and-concrete tribute to the Holiday Inn school of architecture. The baroque old building on Centre Street had been good enough for the Chief, but the army of button-down bureaucrats who had replaced him, and who were making the likes of Captain Pat Chambers obsolete, required more modern digs.

Milroy, on the eleventh floor, had a civilian secretary/receptionist seated outside his glassed-in office. I could see the inspector at his desk and he could see me. The secretary, attractive despite horned-rimmed glasses and pinned-up hair, wanted to know if I had an appointment, and I just nodded to where her boss was waving at me to come in.

I did so, shutting the door behind me. I stuck my hat on the coat tree. Milroy didn't rise, just sat there going over a stack of computer printouts. Without looking at me, he gestured to the chair opposite him, and I sat. As I waited for him to grant me his attention, I took the office in.

It was twice the size of Pat's glassed-in cubicle, with a round table off to one side for conferences. Industrial carpet. A coffee machine. The walls were filled with framed citations of merit and photographs of Milroy with various NYPD chiefs of police over the years as well as every mayor from the last three decades. His desk was neat and arrayed with framed family photos—his pleasant-looking wife and their two clean-cut sons at various ages, the boys as young as grade school and as old as college.

He put the printouts down and worked up something like a smile, one of the few he'd given me over the years. He'd been a good-looking man in his younger days, a freckled, broad-shouldered blond. After his automobile accident twenty years ago, he began to get heavier and his face took on the reddish cast and slightly exploded features of the heavy drinker. Still, his record as a police inspector was commendable, as all the citations attested.

"I hear you pulled one of your fancy self-defense plays last night," he said, his growl more good-natured than usual.

"I did. I'm surprised you didn't come around with Pat to look for loopholes."

He shook his head. "For once I'm on your side, Hammer. Captain Chambers says those two over-the-hill wiseguys were seen at the Chief's nursing home and at the hospital. He feels they were responsible for our friend's murder."

"No question one of them used a knife on the Chief. We'll never know which."

A small smile flashed. "Actually, when you talk to Captain Chambers next, he'll tell you—Rossi had a switchblade in his pocket, and forensics ties it to the Chief's wound. So I guess I owe you a debt of thanks."

"For what?"

"For wrapping this thing up."

"There's still a bow that needs tying on."

"Oh?"

I leaned in. "You see, Inspector . . . the Chief gave me something. Entrusted me with it, you might say. And now I have to make a decision."

His frown was curious, not hostile. "A decision?"

"Yeah. About what to do with it. I'll probably give it twenty-four hours."

The frown deepened into confusion. "Give *what* twenty-four hours?"

"Before deciding what to do. Better to give it to the current chief, or hand it over to the media? I wonder."

"Hand *what* over?"

I glanced around, smiled pleasantly. "Nice office, Inspector. You just moved in, right? And now you're retiring soon, lot of trouble and bother for such a short stay. Still, I guess you gotta enjoy it while you've got it."

"What the hell are you getting at, Hammer?"

I sat back, folded my arms, put an ankle on a knee and got comfy. "I have a little story to share with you, Inspector."

"Hammer, I'm not retiring today. I'm still a busy man."

"Just . . . *humor* me, okay? Our friend the Chief, back before the war, took on the mob like nobody who sat in his chair ever dared before. And at the same time, he cleaned out a whole passel of bent cops."

"Not a new story, Hammer. It's well-known."

"The broad outlines are. But how did he manage it? One thing he would've needed was somebody on the inside—a crooked cop, particularly one close to the mob, who could feed him names and information. He had something on this cop, or else he wouldn't have been able to put the squeeze on. And the Chief filed that away, as a kind of life insurance policy. If anything happened to him, that evidence would come out."

Thick fingers drummed on the desk. "Interesting theory. But also ancient history."

"Some history never gets ancient. Like I was saying to Pat, there's no statute of limitations on murder, for example."

His eyes, a bloodshot sky blue, flared.

I went on: "The Chief, of course, never fully trusted that cop. He couldn't fire him without giving away both of their secrets. They had each made their respective deals with their respective devils. So the Chief kept this cop on staff, kept him close—you know the old saying, 'Keep your friends close, and your enemies closer.'"

Very softly he said, "You don't have anything on me, Hammer."

I looked toward the little desk altar of framed family photos. "The ironic thing is, that crooked cop kept his act clean after that. Never was his reputation sullied thereafter. Won himself a wall full of awards, medals, commendations. Even after the Chief retired, that cop stayed on the straight and narrow. But I bet he never proved himself to the old boy. Never good enough for the Chief to feel he could either turn that evidence over to the now-reformed cop, or just destroy it. So that evidence, that sword of Damocles, it just hung over that poor bastard's head—an old sin that all the new good deeds in the world just couldn't make go away. And as the Chief neared the natural death at a ripe old age that his life insurance policy had bought him, the cop was worried it would all come out. Disgrace. Maybe even jail time. A hero who was suddenly a villain. A proud man with two sons would find that hard to take. Don't blame the guy."

His jaw was set but trembling. "What did he *give* you, Hammer?"

"So the cop reaches out to some old mob cronies and convinces them that what the Chief is holding back is going to ruin what little is left of their own sad, sorry lives. I'm going to guess that the cop didn't tell them to kill the Chief. I'm going to give him the benefit of the doubt that they adlibbed that one. But, hell, it should have occurred to him what they would do—that they'd have to shut the old guy up before making their search."

He was getting flushed. "What did he give you, Hammer? *Where is it?*"

I got the old .38 Police Positive out of my suitcoat pocket and I set in on the desk, right on top of that pile of printouts he'd been reading.

"That's *one* of the things he gave me," I said. "I think he probably wanted you to have it."

Milroy stared down at the old revolver.

"I saw the Chief shoot Gino Madoni with that piece," I said, "when I was a kid. First bad guy that I ever saw shot. And it was up close and personal, let me tell you."

I went over and got my hat and placed a hand on the door knob. "You have several choices, Inspector, including coming after me. Hell, I've even provided the gun. If you want to find me, I'll be at my office this afternoon, the Blue Ribbon restaurant for supper with Captain Chambers, and at my apartment after that. I'm in the book."

His hand was on the gun—not gripping it, just resting on it, like a fire-and-brimstone preacher laying on a healing hand. His face was red now and the lightning bolt scar stood out starkly.

"Tomorrow morning," I said, "I'll turn over what I have to the current chief. That gives you another option—take your chances and take your medicine."

Very quietly he said, "But there's another option."

"There is. A lot of good cops have taken it, for all kinds of reasons. Depression. Family problems. A fatal illness. Men who live by the gun . . . you know the rest. You make the right decision, Inspector, and I won't have to come forward. And I'll get rid of the evidence once and for all."

He glanced up at me. "You'd do that for me?"

"You have my word. But you know something? I believe the Chief wouldn't have hung you out to dry, not after all these years . . . unless you reverted to form and came after him. That gun there? He had it in his hand, under the sheet, in that hospital room. Ready to do what he had to."

Milroy sighed. "Yeah. He was a hell of a guy. I came to respect him. I don't think . . . I don't think I was ever able to gain his."

I shrugged. "Never too late to try."

And I left him there with his thoughts and the gun and all the rest of it.

The gunmetal sky was grumbling. Cloud cover was low and dark with lightning bolts shorting in and out. I was in my raincoat and hat standing outside the Blue Ribbon, as if I were waiting for it to come down after me.

Really, I was waiting for Pat, having already sent Velda inside to grab our regular table. My stomach was grumbling worse than the sky, but some of George's knockwurst would cure my ills, whereas the sky would have to bust itself apart to get over its lousy attitude.

As if the sky had already done that, Pat came running from somewhere, also in raincoat and hat. When he saw me, he slowed and then we stood there while he lit up a Lucky. He was the kind of gentleman who didn't like to smoke at a table in a restaurant when a lady was in the party. But this was something else.

"I'm sorry I'm late, Mike," he said. "All hell's broken loose at the Plaza."

"Yeah?"

"You're not going to believe this, but Milroy went home this afternoon and blew his brains out in his den."

"No."

"He used a gun that once belonged to the Chief. They were really tight, you know. It was probably a gift to him."

"Probably."

Pat drew in smoke, exhaled it, sending a small blue cloud up to join the big bad black ones. "He left a note. Turns out he had a brain tumor. Been having blinding headaches and just couldn't take it anymore."

"Pity. Will there be an autopsy?"

"No. What the hell for?" Then he eyed me sideways with the usual suspicion. "You don't sniff foul play, do you, Mike? Some suicides really *are* suicides, you know."

"No, no. You're right."

"Probably the Chief's murder sent him over the edge. You never really know people, do you?" He sighed and pitched the cigarette sparking toward the street. "Velda inside?"

"Yeah. Go in and join her, will you? Something I need to take care of."

"Sure."

Pat went in.

The sky came apart in pieces, thunder like cannonfire, rain sheeting down. I slipped under the Blue Ribbon canopy and still got wet, watching jagged white streaks carve the deep black smoke of it.

I walked through the downpour to the curb, let the key bounce in the palm of my hand a few times, then tossed it into the gutter, where the rush of water carried it to the sewer and gone.

"So long, Chief," I said, and went inside.

A DANGEROUS CAT

Somebody had let the cat out.

It jumped off its perch by the hallway window outside my apartment and came over to rub itself against my legs with the tip of its tail making little sexy twitches of hello.

Maybe the gray-and-white female felt when that instinctive sense of survival hit me, because the animal drew back a second, gave a soundless meow and stiff-legged itself to the door, waiting for me to move.

A few hours ago, that cat—who had adopted me when the neighbors across the way left her behind—had been locked inside my apartment and nobody but me had the keys.

Well, me and Velda, my secretary and partner in Michael Hammer Investigations. She lived in the building, too. But I'd just come down from her apartment, where we'd shared breakfast.

That makes three tries, I thought, the hair on the back of my neck standing up like I was the cat. *The other two times hadn't been accidents or coincidences at all.*

No jimmy marks on the door frame or around the lock, no signs of forcible entry evident, but the cat was out here, and that meant somebody had been in there.

I took out the .45, jacked a shell into the chamber and

worked my key in the slot and opened the door. It was a steel fireproof job and I got well down under any logical line of fire, if the setup was meant for sudden ambush.

But that damn cat got in ahead of me and I could tell right away that the place was empty, otherwise puss would have stuck her tail up in immediate alert.

All she did was run for the kitchenette milk bowl as I closed the door, probed the area, then holstered the .45 and picked up the phone on the little table by my recliner facing the TV.

Captain Pat Chambers of the NYPD was still at his desk, getting the paperwork out on the Lightener case, and however tired his hello might sound, it was good to hear.

"It's Mike, buddy. Feel like some action?"

"Knock it off, pal. You know my ass is dragging after yesterday."

"Humor me, anyway."

I could hear his chair creak as he sat back. "Okay, consider yourself humored. Now what?"

"Turns out somebody doesn't like me."

A weary chuckle. "And this is news?"

"Not so much. I've been set up for a kill before."

This time the creak of the chair meant he was sitting forward. "So what's different this time around?"

"What's different is there's no reason for it."

His voice shifted into concern-tinged professionalism. "You've been around too damn long, Mike, to get easily rattled. What's got your hackles up?"

The tabby came out licking milk from its chops.

I answered his question with one of my own: "You know anybody out at Kennedy who works with sniffers?"

"Dogs, Mike?"

"Dogs, Pat."

"Well, Bill Champlin works with the grass variety. They can point out everything from daisies to hashish, but what—"

"I mean, the ones who go after nitro derivatives."

He let a pause go by before saying, "Shit. Only one I know at all is Toby Verez. Hell, man, I'm Homicide. I only ran into him a few times."

"Run into him again, Pat, then haul his ass up here. Like now."

"What are you *talking* about, Mike?"

I said it nice and slow. "This building is a first-class establishment leasing to a hundred well-connected tenants. Let it blow sky-high and your department is going to be balls deep in trouble. Good enough for a starter?"

"You lay it on pretty heavy, pal," he said.

"I damn well mean to," I told him. "But don't make a production out of it. No bomb squad. Just a talented pooch and his handler. We don't need any panic starting."

"Hell, if you're really onto something, I should get that building evacuated."

"That can happen soon enough. Let's make sure my instincts are right before we make suckers out of both of us."

It took Big Nell twenty seconds to find the blast.

The sleek black Lab zeroed in on the second drawer of the dresser like a falcon creaming a pigeon.

I'd waited for them down on the street, where Pat and Toby Verez suggested I stay. I said if the dog told me to, I would. But the pooch had no opinion and we went up.

After easing out the top drawer, Toby looked down at the contents of the second drawer, which included eight sticks of

Atlas dynamite neatly taped together, triggered to go off the next time I changed my underwear.

I damn near needed a change now.

Toby and Big Nell looked at me with big brown eyes. "By the book," Toby said, "we call the bomb squad now."

"For something this simple?"

Before he could answer, I stuck my hand down and lifted the package while everybody but me and Big Nell gasped. Soon Toby was chopping off the igniter wires, and then he brought out the load. The Lab supervised, slobbering all over the rug, a breach of etiquette I was happy to overlook.

Eight sticks of dynamite that would have left me a misty spray in the wreckage of the building's top three stories turned to rubble raining down to halt weekend traffic below.

Pat moved across the bedroom to join us and said, "You were right, Mike. Somebody doesn't like you."

"You surprised?"

My big, rangy cop friend looked cool and professional in a suit that didn't betray the long hours he'd worked yesterday on a matter of mutual interest.

Pat nodded toward the dresser, in front of which Toby was rewarding the dog with a treat and some neck scratching. The dynamite had already been closed into a padded carrier that made the worst picnic basket you ever dug into.

"You know how close you came, buddy?"

I grunted. "Not even hardly. I smelled it first, didn't I?"

"And here I thought the dog did."

"She just pinpointed it."

Toby and his K-9 waited patiently as Pat and I went over to confer in hushed tones across the room. "Mike, you know this has to go on a report."

"Certainly," I said.

"Okay. As the reporting officer, I have to ask—you have an explanation for this?"

I shrugged. "You already gave me one. Somebody doesn't like me."

"Spare me the horseshit."

I grinned at him. "Now maybe you'll take it seriously, what I told you at lunch yesterday."

He made a face, his hands on his hips. "A car almost running you down? That's unusual in New York?"

"Unusual enough to get my attention, when it's deliberate. And that was just the first try."

He was shaking his head. "So you got winged in a shootout. Stop hanging around those damn low-class joints that are always getting held up."

"Pat, damn it, I've been shot at before. If I hadn't swung around on that barstool, when the bartender and that ski-masked non-customer started trading rounds, I'd have had an incoming in the back of the head instead of a crease across the chest." I took a deep breath, as something clicked into place. "*That* explains those eight sticks."

"How so?"

"Think about it. The other night, at that bar . . . that was supposed to be a hit, Pat, disguised as a hold-up. I was supposed to get it in the back of the head. But after I hit the deck, I threw a shot at the guy as he ran out. He was lucky he didn't buy it."

"And you weren't?"

"That was meant to be a hit, Pat. But the guy who tried it decided up close and personal was no way to deal with Mike Hammer."

He rubbed his eyes. "I hate it when you talk about yourself in the third person." He sighed and looked right at me. "What are you working on?"

I waved at the air. "Nothing, that's what. I took two weeks vacation down in Miami with Hy Gardner, then attended that P.I. convention in Vegas . . . and before that I was tied up in a couple of industrials and organized a security deal for Delaney."

"Mike . . . you have more contacts on the street than all the detectives on the PD put together. *Nobody* clued you in?"

"Nobody. Nothing. If I was hot, I'd have heard."

"And you haven't? *Really* haven't?"

"Shit, Pat, I'm not holding out on you. I called you in, didn't I?"

He gestured toward the dresser. "Then why the eight-stick sendoff? That's one hell of a way to wave goodbye."

"Pretty damn definite, though."

I glanced over at Toby. He was holding the dog back so it wouldn't go after the cat. Then that crazy pussy decided to go up and smell him and when he growled, she let him have a swipe across the nostrils and walked away with her tail swishing a *Screw you, dog.*

Some attitude. I liked her.

Monday just before noon I took Velda to the Blue Ribbon Restaurant on West 44th Street between Sixth and Seventh Avenues. George, the owner, served up the best German food in Manhattan, and always saw to it I got my special table in a corner nook overseen by framed celebrity photos. Dark wood gave the place warmth and the lighting was nicely subdued, even at lunch.

The raven tresses of her sleek pageboy brushing her shoulders, my secretary was tall and curvy but no overgrown baby doll—she carried a P.I. ticket in her wallet and a .32 in her purse. In that simple pale yellow silk blouse and brown pencil skirt, she looked sexier than Ann Corio at the end of her act.

Velda knew all about my booby-trapped dresser and we'd gone over it plenty of times yesterday in her apartment, just two floors above mine. But not a word on the subject had been exchanged all morning. Still, I could see it was bugging her.

"Listen," she said, nibbling at a shrimp salad while I gobbled knockwurst, "while you were making your phone calls, on that insurance job, I was digging through our special file."

"You mean the file of my fan club members?"

"Right, if by that you mean scum you sent up or killed. And you know Pat helps me keep close tabs on 'friends' of yours who've been sprung from Sing Sing lately."

I chewed sauerkraut. "What would I do without you two looking after my interests?"

She ignored that, spearing a shrimp. "I also keep track of those you've jugged or buried who have the kind of family members who might seek revenge."

I grinned at her. "Somebody taking vengeance out on me? That's what they call irony, right? Or is it karma?"

"For a guy who likes to get even," she said, with a humorless smirk, "you're a little cavalier about the loved ones of dearly departeds who you made that way."

"Okay, so you looked through the file. Come up with anything?"

She shook her head and scythes of dark hair swung. "It's been two or three years since we got into anything that wasn't paying business. For such a hardass, you've been leading a downright respectable, even boring existence lately."

I buttered a hard roll. "Boring except for a phony hit-and-run, that staged shootout, and eight sticks of dynamite."

"Except for those." She leaned forward, urgency in the dark eyes. "We have to dig deeper, Mike. Put everything else on hold and make keeping you alive our top priority. You're not like that cat of yours—you don't have nine lives."

"I don't have a cat, either."

"You don't? What would you call it?"

I swallowed a nice foamy mouthful of Pabst. "Cat-sitting till I can find a nice home for the thing. There's got to be some family with kids out there who would love to have a pet like that."

"If not," she said, "what will you do with it? Take a ride in the country and dump it somewhere?"

"No."

"Toss it in an alley by a bunch of garbage cans, maybe? Or in a bag off a bridge?"

"Hell no."

Her smile was sly and faintly mocking. "Then answer me this, Mike. Did you round up a litter box for the animal?"

"Yeah. She has to crap, doesn't she?"

"Did you buy cat chow for her? Do you put milk down for her?"

"Yeah, so what?"

"So, Mike," she said, and sipped coffee, "*you* have a cat."

Pat Chambers rolled in. I'd told him we'd be lunching here and to join us. He couldn't make the meal but said he'd stop by, anyway.

He pulled up a chair, a pilsner automatically delivered to

him, and he said, "No fingerprints anywhere on that present your secret admirer left you."

I frowned. "You took fingerprints all over my place. Didn't you get anything?"

He shook his head. "Just yours and Velda's and what turned out to be your cleaning lady. What does that tell you?"

"That when it comes to tracking down cleaning ladies, you don't need any help from me."

"Laugh it off, Mike. Somebody wants you dead. And that lack of prints screams professional. Also, we canvassed your building and nobody saw anything or anybody suspicious."

I shrugged, took another gulp of beer. "What did Toby have to say about that surprise package?"

"That it was simple but deadly, and showed skills. Again, likely a pro job. I'll ask you one more time, Mike. What do you make of this?"

I leaned back. "Same as you. Somebody wants me dead."

"Any idea who?"

"Not a clue."

"Don't get cute."

"If what you're getting at, buddy, is that all of this indicates somebody hiring a kill, I won't argue. These tries have been sophisticated, and they've escalated. The hit-and-run could've been written off as an accident. That saloon shootout might have been a coincidence, just Mike Hammer frequenting a rough slopchute and getting tagged. A fitting end for a mur-derous thug who passes himself off as a private eye."

Pat grumbled, "Third person again."

I sat forward. "But this latest attempt, trying to make me go boom—all pretense has been dropped of anything but murder, and the kind of murder that indicates somebody is getting desperate."

Velda said, "But if that explosion had happened, maybe it wouldn't have been tracked to your apartment. Maybe it would've been written off as a gas leak incident. And that, too, would be seen as a coincidence."

"I don't think so," I said. "Pat, your forensics boys would've been able to pinpoint where that explosion started, right?"

"Most likely," he said with a nod.

"No," I said to Velda, "I think somebody is past caring about making my murder look like something else. I think somebody's going to take a shot at me, maybe not hiring it done this time. But that somebody's overlooking one small item."

"Which is?" Velda asked.

Pat was smirking. He wouldn't rise to that bait.

"I shoot back," I said.

The afternoon had barely begun when Velda slipped into my office and said, "We've got a walk-in. I think you should see him."

"What happened to putting everything on hold?"

She leaned a hand on my desk. "I've been going over that file of possibles again, and I may have a lead or two in a few hours, but not till then. Also, Pat gave me some names on the Lightener case to check up on."

I waved that off. "The poor young husband killed the rich older wife and got caught. That's the beginning and the end."

"He has relatives. Any time there are relatives, these things can come back on you." She nodded toward the outer office. "But right now, why not help this fella?"

"The walk-in? You look like somebody's been pulling your heart strings."

Her frown dripped sympathy. "Just talk to him, Mike. His name is Oliver Roland, and he's from Des Moines."

"He would be."

She gave me the sad eyes, like a cat begging for dinner. "Please?"

So I had her send the guy in.

He was of medium size in a light brown suit that was not cheap, and the dark blue tie was silk. For all the crispness of his clothing, he had a rumpled look—dark circles under bloodshot brown eyes, thinning blond hair that a brush or comb hadn't tamed. He was an odd combination of fresh and stale.

I gestured to the client's chair and he gave me a twitch of a smile, nodded and sat.

"Thank you for seeing me, Mr. Hammer." The voice was mid-range and tiredness was in it. The way he slumped in the chair played into that. "I didn't know where else to turn."

"Why is that, Mr. Roland?"

He sighed. His oblong face was droopy with sadness. "The police won't be interested. Alice is of age, and she left home willingly."

"Alice."

He nodded. "My sister. She and I live . . . lived . . . with my mother back in Des Moines. Our *sickly* mother, I should say. I think I leaned a little too hard on Alice, taking care of Mother . . . I work for an insurance company, with long and sometimes unpredictable hours, and since Alice was out of high school, I thought it was . . . *reasonable* to have her help look after Mother."

"Sounds like it to me. But maybe not to her—she left home?"

He closed his eyes like a man fighting a headache. Then he

opened them and said, "Yes. Six months ago. Mother has since
. . . Mother passed away three months after Alice left. I don't
blame Alice for that in any way. She had . . . aspirations, Alice
did. Had."

Why the past tense? I wondered. But I let him go on at his
own speed.

"Alice is a very pretty girl." He got a photo from his inside
pocket and pushed it across to me.

He wasn't exaggerating—she was a lovely blue-eyed blonde
in a light blue shift, so short it could have been a man's shirt.
Slender, on the flat-chested side, but with legs that went on
forever.

"How old is she here?" I asked.

"Seventeen. She still looked like that when she went away.
She left a note and said she'd be in touch, but she never called
or wrote."

"You said aspirations. What kind?"

Another sigh, this one heavy with frustration. "Alice was
active in drama and in music. She was a good high school
actress and a pleasant singer, but . . . Mr. Hammer, the idea
that she could come to New York and make it in show business, well . . . it's almost absurd."

"A lot of young ones have tried." *And gotten old in a hurry.*
"And it's been six months? Why start looking for her now, Mr.
Roland? That's what you're doing, isn't it?"

He sat forward. "Actually, I wasn't looking for her. A friend
of mine in the insurance business was in New York for a convention last week, and said he saw her. Spotted her on the
street with some other girls and women who were very hard-
looking. Overly made-up. Skimpy but flashy attire."

It wasn't a punch worth pulling. "You figure she's hooking?"

He swallowed and looked at the hands he'd folded in his lap. "I think so, yes. Everybody knows prostitution is something a lot of girls . . . runaways . . . get into."

"But she didn't run away. She was of voting age and she split of her own accord."

He nodded glumly. "That's right. That's why the police are of no use."

"But you think I might be?"

Some life came into his eyes. "I read an article about you in a true-detective magazine. It made you sound smart and tough, not afraid of anything. And said that you know Manhattan better than anybody else in the private eye 'game.'"

"Maybe they exaggerated."

He shook his head. "I don't think so. The article covered a lot of your cases. You sound like the genuine article to me, Mr. Hammer. You would know where to look for her, and you wouldn't be afraid to go looking there, either."

"There are a lot of places to look, Mr. Roland. Prostitution is a pretty thriving business in this town."

"But . . . you could do it, right?"

I hadn't answered when he shoved a wad of bills on the desk, right next to Alice's picture.

"That's a thousand-dollar cash retainer, Mr. Hammer."

"That will buy you a week but won't cover expenses."

"I have more money. I can go as high as ten thousand. Can you find her in the time that would buy?"

"Possibly. But what then? She's of age and kidnapping's illegal, even in this town."

The bloodshot eyes were moist, haunted. "Just find her and lead me to her. If I could have a chance to talk to her . . . tell her Mother has passed . . . that there's a better life waiting for her back home, and that I would *never* judge her. Just want to . . . to save her from this terrible life."

"Is your conventioneer friend certain it was Alice he saw?" I skipped asking how the pal happened to be in the proximity of a bunch of doxies.

The client nodded. "He was . . . Stan's her godfather. It was her."

"Did he say where he saw her?"

"He said a side street off Times Square. That's all he could say."

That sounded right.

"Would you look for her, Mr. Hammer?"

"Sure," I said. "But there's a condition."

"Name it."

"I have to be with you when you meet up with her. If I lead you to her, I stick around for the family reunion."

"Why?"

"Because I won't be party to a kidnapping. If she's willing to talk with you, and reacts well to seeing you, fine. But if she wants to be left alone, we have to respect that. Understood?"

He nodded a bunch of times. "Understood. Thank you, Mr. Hammer. You don't know what this means to me."

Getting to his feet, he extended a hand. I got up and shook it. The shake was firmer than I'd expected.

"When will you get started?"

"First thing tomorrow. I have another matter to attend to this afternoon and evening. Where can I get in touch with you?"

"Ritz-Carlton. Your secretary has the details."

He grinned and some of the tiredness drained away.

"You've made me very happy, Mr. Hammer."

"Let's not get ahead of ourselves, Mr. Roland."

But a man who had dragged in went out with spring in his step.

I sat on the edge of Velda's desk, craning to look back at her. "Find anything?"

She nodded, file cards spread out on her desk like she was reading Tarot. "Two decent possibilities. Remember Shriver, the pedophile you got sent up who was killed in a Sing Sing shower?"

"Even that didn't get him clean. Sure. But his family was straight, as I recall. Strictly middle-class."

Her eyebrows went up. "Well, he has an uncle who was a Green Beret, and did a year, post-Nam, for beating up a long-hair in a Queens bar."

"Okay. We'll talk to him."

"And there's the Craig case. The embezzler?"

I shrugged. "We got the goods and he hanged himself. I didn't even waste a bullet. And that was an upper middle-class family."

"Maybe so, but his wife's father is a welder in Brooklyn who did time for armed robbery twenty years ago."

I made a face. "That seems a little thin. But we should chat him up, too, I suppose."

"We can take off now."

She wouldn't be calling first—these were the kind of visits that worked better just dropping by.

"I got nothing else on," I said, flipping a hand, "but our new client. And he isn't expecting anything out of us till tomorrow, anyway. Speaking of which . . ."

From a suitcoat pocket I got out the grand in hundreds Roland had given me and handed them over.

"I'll put this in the safe," she said, thumbing through the green. Shifting gears, she said, "Do you think we can find his sister for him?"

I shrugged. "If she hasn't stuck a needle in her arm too many times, or bought it from her pimp or a john? A good possibility." From my other jacket pocket I gave her the photo of Alice Roland. "Get a print of this made first thing tomorrow. Send one over to Pat to run past the Vice boys. Then in the afternoon we'll both head over to Times Square for a little safari."

"The girls around there like you," she said wryly. "You'll do fine. But what about me?"

"Maybe you can buy some slutty threads and just, you know, infiltrate. But I'll have to inspect your wardrobe to make sure you're up to snuff."

"You wish," she said, but she was smiling.

Then we headed out to Queens.

But we got nowhere in particular, in Queens or Brooklyn, either.

The pedophile's ex–Green Beret uncle, a garage mechanic who we caught up with at a Texaco station, seemed at first a possibility, judging by the way he patted an open palm with the working end of a wrench.

Still, when he claimed he thought his nephew got what he deserved, he seemed to be leveling. Velda asked him about the hippie kid he'd throttled in that bar and he got embarrassed.

"I ain't proud of that," he said, a big guy whose paunch didn't take anything away from his linebacker build. "I was on the sauce in them days but I dried out in stir. That's one thing that beats the A.A. all to hell."

"What is?" I asked.

"Sing Sing."

The welder in Brooklyn was in his driveway washing his car. He was another bruiser gone slightly to seed, though where the Green Beret had been in his forties, this guy was sixty, easy.

He was standoffish at first, but he took in our P.I. tickets with wide eyes, and took Velda in with wider eyes. She smiled at him and said something or other, and it softened him up. Or maybe got him hard.

Either way it worked, and we soon learned there was no love lost between him and his dead son-in-law.

"Creep left my little Lois up a creek without a paddle. If he hadn't hung himself, I'd have strangled the little scumbag when he got out. Thank God Lois found a better man and things've turned around for her."

And when he realized I was the guy who'd nailed the son-in-law for that insurance company, he pumped my hand and grinned at me, like I'd done him the biggest turn ever.

Back in Manhattan, we stopped at P. J. Moriarty's on Sixth and Fifty-Second where I bought Velda a dainty little steak and myself a big rare slab of one. I cut into mine and let the blood run as Velda said, "We could head over to Times Square now, you know."

I shook my head. "I don't want to go bothering working girls during prime time. They'll be looser lipped in the afternoon. Anyway, we haven't bought you those special clothes yet."

"Keep dreaming." She nibbled a delicate bite of dead bovine, then admitted, "I'm pretty tired, anyway. Crawling around Queens and Brooklyn can take it out of a girl."

I nodded. "We'll find Roland's missing sister, if she's in

town to be found. And we won't have to dip into that other nine grand he flashed at me, either."

So we headed back to our apartment building, where she let me out on my floor like a good little elevator operator and went on up to hers.

How tired I was hit me the second I stepped into my apartment, but before I could flop into my recliner, the cat was clawing at my pants leg, her purrs more like growls as she demanded her dinner. In the kitchenette, I poured some chow into a bowl and gave her a dish of water. She looked up at me accusingly.

"Milk's a treat," I said. "Sometimes you got to get by on just plain water."

She gave me a look, but she settled.

I settled, too, in my recliner, after divesting myself of my suitcoat, shoulder-holstered .45, and shoes. I was trying to decide whether to read the funnies or see what the tube had to offer when the phone on the stand at my right trilled at me.

"Yeah," I said into the receiver. If they wanted "Hammer speaking," they had to call the office.

"Mr. Hammer? It's Oliver Roland."

I sat up, spurred by the urgency in his voice.

"I've seen her, Mr. Hammer! I spotted Alice. Right off Times Square, like my friend said."

"Well, that's great. That's fine. But I'd rather you not approach her till I'm around."

"That's why I'm calling. I don't dare talk to her."

"Why not?"

"There's a big black gentleman in flashy clothes with her. I think he's her pimp. She's talking to him and they aren't . . . aren't getting along."

140

If it hadn't sounded so serious, I might have been amused. Only an out-of-towner from Des Moines would have said all of that, that way.

"Stay away from them, Mr. Roland. Where are you exactly?"

He told me.

"Good. I can be there in fifteen minutes. Just stay away from them."

He said all right, then thanked me profusely.

"I haven't done anything yet," I said.

I hung up, got up, shook my head, then went into the kitchen and threw some water on my face. The cat, still eating, looked up at me with feline disdain. Imagine making her drink water and not milk.

So I got back into my shoes and put on the shoulder holster, after checking the action on the .45, jacking one into the chamber and clicking off the safety. Wearing the gun like that didn't exactly seem prudent—till some asshole pulled on you.

And I was on my way to discuss this and that with a big black pimp. I mean, gentleman.

I slipped my suitcoat on as I made the trip to the door, and when I opened it, Oliver Roland was standing there with a .38 revolver in his fist.

And he didn't look at all tired.

"Inside, Hammer," he said, his voice cold and hard, unrecognizable from the concerned tremble of earlier today. Only the bloodshot eyes were the same. "Hands up and empty."

I stepped back inside, obeying his instructions.

"You're damn good," I said. "I bought your story, hook, line and sinker, though I admit the grand sold it. What did you do just now, call me from the house phone?"

When the door was closed behind us, he ignored my question and said, "That fabled .45 of yours? Use two fingers to pluck it out and drop it. Nice and easy, so it doesn't go off when it hits the floor."

I'm fast but not fast enough when a .38 is leveled at me. Again, I did as I was told.

"Since you're a pro," I said, "you won't mind telling me who hired you."

"I'm no pro," he said proudly, upper lip pulled back in a ghastly smile. "This is *my* kill, all mine. In a way, I'm glad the first two tries failed. Those I hired. Then I knew it was time to take things into my own hands."

"*Two* tries? What about that lovely bomb tucked in with my jockeys?"

"That was me." His nose twitched. He blinked. He swallowed. "I was a demo man with the Marines in Nam. I figured if a job was worth doing . . . you know the rest."

"And now it's up close and personal."

He nodded, his smile a curdled thing. He was still in that crisp suit but he no longer looked stale at all. It had all been an act, a story he concocted. No Alice. Just a damn good sell job.

He rubbed his nose with his free hand, then nodded past me. "Sit in that recliner, Hammer. Turn it facing the couch."

I did so.

"We're going to sit and talk. I want you to think about what's coming, which is a .38 dum dum in the belly, so you can die just as slow as my brother."

He was backing slowly over to the couch, keeping the weapon poised to shoot.

"Then you ought to use my .45," I said easily, hands still shoulder high. "That's what I use for maximum discomfort."

"You are a cold son of a bitch," he said, and sat on the couch, facing me, sitting forward, the gun honed right at my belly. "You know, I really did read up on you in those detective magazines. I wanted to know all about the bastard who killed my brother."

"I told you those mags exaggerated things. I'm really a pussycat."

Perfectly on cue, the cat jumped on the couch and Roland looked at it with something approaching terror.

And then he sneezed.

I was on him right now and turned that .38 in his hand upward so that he was staring into the barrel and the barrel was staring right back, and when I pressed my finger over his and triggered the weapon, I gave him a grin to take with him as orange flame blossomed in his face and the inside of his skull ruined my curtains.

They were old and dirty, anyway.

The cat had disappeared at the gun shot, but I was grateful to it just the same. I'd fix her up with a bowl of milk when I caught my breath.

I understood now that I'd been right: somebody had *let the cat out. Not accidentally, but on purpose. Because Roland was allergic. Those bloodshot eyes weren't for the imaginary Alice after all.*

I slumped into the recliner, and was reaching for the phone to call Pat when I heard the key work in the door. I glanced around at Velda rushing in, in her white terry bathrobe, .32 in hand. The sound of the gunshot had carried two floors, and she knew it wasn't any backfire.

"My God, Mike," she said, coming to an abrupt stop beside me. "That's our client!"

"Yeah. It was all a bunch of bull. There is no Alice, just a guy after revenge . . . like what you said this would be about."

The big brown eyes were at their biggest. "*Revenge?* Revenge for what?"

"For killing his brother."

"Who . . . ? Hell, Mike, who *was* his brother, anyway?"

I shrugged.

"I didn't ask," I said.

IT'S IN THE BOOK

Cops always come in twos. One will knock on the door, but a pair will come in, a duet on hand in case you get rowdy. One uniform drives the squad car, the other answers the radio. One plainclothes dick asks the questions, the other takes the notes. Sometimes I think the only time they go solo is to the dentist. Or to bed. Or to kill themselves.

I went out into the outer office where a client had been waiting for ten minutes for me to get off the phone. A woman had come in after him, but this six-footer was first and I nodded in his direction, but he was already on his feet, brown shoes, brown suit, brown eyes, brown hair. It was a relief his name wasn't Brown.

Velda, the raven-haired ex-cop who is both my secretary and partner, gave me a sideways look from her reception desk. Something tickled one corner of her pretty mouth and her dark eyes were amused.

I said, "I can see you now, Mr. Hanson."

Mr. Hanson nodded back. There was no nervous smile, no anxiety in his manner at all. Generally, anybody needing a private investigator is not at ease. For a fraction of a second, like Velda, I let my eyes laugh at him—at the obviousness of who and what he was. Then I walked toward him and he extended a

145

hand for me to shake, but I moved right past, going to the door and pulling it open.

His partner was standing just to my left with his back to the wall, like a sentry, hands clasped behind his back. He was a little smaller than Hanson, wearing a different shade of brown, going wild with a tie of yellow and white stripes. Of course, he was younger, maybe thirty where his partner was pushing forty.

"Why don't you come in and join your buddy," I said, and made an after-you gesture.

This one didn't smile either. He simply gave me a long look and, without nodding or saying a word, stepped inside and walked up and stood beside Hanson, like they were sharing the wrong end of a firing squad.

After I closed the door, I saw Velda hiding a grin as I took the cops into my private office and got behind the desk.

I waved at the clients' chairs and invited them to sit down. But cops don't like invitations and they stayed on their feet.

Rocking back, I said, "You fellas aren't flashing any warrants, meaning this isn't a search party or an arrest. So have a seat."

Reluctantly, they did.

Hanson's partner, who looked like his feelings had been hurt, said, "How'd you make us?"

I don't know how to give enigmatic looks, so I said, "Come off it."

"We could be businessmen."

"Businessmen don't wear guns on their hips, or if they do, they could afford a suit tailored for it. You're too clean-cut to be hoods, but not enough to be feds. You're either NYPD or visiting badges from Jersey."

This time they looked at each other and Hanson shrugged.

Why fight it? They were cops with a job to do—this was nothing personal. He casually reached in a side suitcoat pocket and flicked a folded hundred-dollar bill onto the desk as if leaving a generous tip.

"Okay," I said. "You have my attention."

"We want to hire you."

The way he hated saying it made it tough for me to keep a straight face. "Who is we?"

"You said it before," Hanson said. "NYPD." *He almost choked, getting that out.*

I pointed at the bill on the desktop. "Why the money?"

"To keep this matter legal. To insure confidentiality. Under your licensing arrangement with the state of New York, you guarantee that by acceptance of payment."

"And if I reject the offer?"

For a moment I thought both of them would smile, but they stifled the effort even if their eyes bore a hint of relief.

Interesting—they wanted *me to pass.*

So I picked up the bill, filled out a receipt, and handed it to Hanson. He looked at it carefully, folded it, and tucked it into his wallet.

"What's this all about?" I asked them.

Hanson composed himself and folded his hands in his lap. They were big hands, but flexible. Hands that had been around. He said, "This was *not* the department's idea."

"I didn't think so."

He took a few moments to look for the words. "I'm sure you know, Hammer, that there are people in government who have more clout than police chiefs or mayors."

I nodded. He didn't have to spell it out. Hell, we both knew what he was getting at.

There was the briefest pause and his eyes went to my phone and then around the room. Before he could ask, I said, "Yes, I'm wired to record client interviews . . . no, I didn't hit the switch. You're fine."

But they glanced at each other nervously just the same.

I said, "If you're that worried, we can take it outside . . . onto the street, where we can talk."

Hanson nodded, already getting up. "Let's do it that way then."

The three of us went into the outer office. I paused to speak to our waiting client, explaining that Velda, as the firm's other investigator, would take her information, but that on my return I'd give the matter my full attention. That satisfied the prospective client.

But as for Velda, a vision in a white blouse and black skirt, any amusement was gone from her eyes now that she saw I was heading out with this pair of obvious coppers.

We used the back door to the semi-private staircase the janitor used for emptying the trash, and went down to the street. There you can talk. Traffic and pedestrians jam up microphones, movement keeps you away from listening ears, and stuck in the midst of all those people, you have the greatest privacy in the world.

We strolled. It was a sunny spring morning but cool.

A block and a half later, Hanson said, "A United States senator is in Manhattan to be part of a United Nations conference."

"One of those dirty jobs somebody's gotta do, I suppose."

"While he's in town, there's an item the senator would like you to recover."

Suddenly this didn't sound so big-time, senator or not.

I frowned. "What's this, a simple robbery?"

"No. There's nothing 'simple' about this situation. But there are aspects of it that make you . . . ideal."

My God, he hated to admit that.

I said, "Your people have already been on it?"

"No."

"Why not?"

"Not your concern, Hammer."

Not my concern?

We stopped at a red light at the street corner, and I asked, "Where's the FBI in this, if there's investigating to do? A U.S. senator ought to be able to pull those strings."

"This is a local affair. Strictly New York."

The light changed and we started ambling across the intersection in the thick of other pedestrians. There was something strange about the term Hanson used—"recovery." If not a robbery, was this mystery item something simply . . . lost? Or maybe I was expected to steal something. I deliberately slowed the pace and started looking in store windows.

Hanson said, "You haven't asked who the senator is."

"You said it was local. So that narrows it to two."

"And you're not curious which one?"

"Nope."

Hanson frowned. "Why not?"

"Because you'll tell me when you're ready, or I'll get to meet him myself."

No exasperation showed in the cop's face, and not even in his tone. Strictly in his words: "What kind of private investigator are you, Hammer? Don't you have any questions at all?"

I stopped abruptly, turning my back to a display window and gave them each a look. Anybody going past would have thought we were just three friends discussing where to grab a bite or a quick drink. Only someone knowledgeable would have seen that the way we stood or moved was designed to keep the bulk of a gun well-concealed under suitcoats, and the expressions we wore were strictly for the passerby audience.

I said, "No wonder you guys are pissed off. With all the expertise of the NYPD, the senator decides to call *me* in to find a missing geegaw for you. That's worth a horse laugh."

This time Hanson did choke a little bit. "This . . . 'geegaw' may be small in size, Hammer, but it's causing rumbles from way up top."

"Obviously all the way up to the senator's office."

Hanson said nothing, but that was an answer in itself.

"What's higher than that?"

And it hit me.

It was crazy, but I heard myself asking the question: "Not . . . the President?"

Hanson swallowed. Then he shrugged again. "I didn't say that, Hammer. But . . . he's top dog, isn't he?"

I grunted out a laugh. "Not *these* days he isn't."

Maybe if they had been feds, I'd have been accused of treason or sedition or stupidity. But these two—well, Hanson, at least—knew the answer already. I gave it to them anyway.

"These days," I said, "political parties and bankrollers and lobbyists call the shots. No matter how important the pol, he's still a chess piece for money to move around. That includes the big man in the Oval Office."

Hanson's partner chimed in: "That's a cynical point of view, Hammer."

A kid on a skateboard wheeled around the corner. When he'd passed, I said, "What kind of recovery job rates this kind of pressure?"

We started walking again.

Hanson said, "It's there, so who cares. We're all just pawns, right, Hammer? Come on. Let's go."

"Where?"

"To see the senator," he said.

We might have been seated in the sumptuous living room of a Westchester mansion, considering the overstuffed furnishings, the burnished wood, the Oriental carpet. But this was the Presidential suite of the Hotel St. Moritz on Central Park South.

My host, seated in an armchair fit for a king, was not the president, merely a United States senator serving his third consecutive term. And Senator Hugh Boylan, a big pale fleshy man with a Leprechaun twinkle, looked as out of place here as I did. His off-white seersucker suit and carelessly knotted blue-and-red striped tie went well with shaggy gray hair that was at least a week past due for a haircut. His eyebrows were thick dark sideways exclamation points, a masculine contrast to a plumply sensuous mouth.

He had seen to it that we both had beers to drink. Bottles, not poured glasses, a nice common-man touch. Both brews rested without coasters on the low-slung marble coffee table between us, where I'd also tossed my hat. I was seated on a nearby couch with more well-upholstered curves than a high-ticket call girl.

The senator sat forward, his light blue eyes gently hooded and heavily red-streaked. He gestured with a thick-fingered hand whose softness belied a dirt-poor upbringing. His days as a longshoreman were far behind him.

"Odd that we've never met, Mr. Hammer, over all these

years." His voice was rich and thick, like Guinness pouring into a glass. "Perhaps it's because we don't share the same politics."

"I don't have any politics, Senator."

Those Groucho eyebrows climbed toward a shaggy fore-lock. "You were famously associated with my conservative colleague, Senator Jasper—there was that rather notorious incident in Russia when you accompanied him as a body-guard."

"That was just a job, sir."

"Then perhaps you won't have any objection to doing a job for a public servant of . . . a *liberal* persuasion."

"As long as you don't try to persuade me, Senator."

"Fair enough," he said with a chuckle, and settled back in the chair, tenting his fingers. "I would hope as a resident of our great state that you might have observed that I fight for my constituency, and try to leave partisan politics out of it. That I've often been at odds with my party for the good of the people."

"Senator, you don't have to sell me. No offense, but I haven't voted in years."

A smile twitched in one corner of his fleshy face. "I am only hoping that you don't view me as an adversary. That you might have some small regard for my efforts."

"You're honest and you're a fighter. That goes a good distance with me."

His pale cheeks flushed red. *Had I struck a nerve without intending?*

"I appreciate that," he said quietly.

Sunshine was filtering through sheer curtains, exposing dust motes—even the St. Moritz had dust. Horns honked below, but faintly, the city out there paying no heed to a venerable public servant and an erstwhile tabloid hero.

"Nicholas Giraldi died last night," he said.

What the hell?

Don Nicholas Giraldi, head of New York's so-called sixth Mafia family, had died in his sleep yesterday in his private room at St. Luke's Hospital. It had been in the evening papers and all over the media—"Old Nic," that most benign of a very un-benign breed, finally gone.

"I heard," I said.

His smile was like a priest's, blessing a recalcitrant parishioner. "You knew him. There are rumors that you even did jobs for him occasionally. That he trusted you."

I sipped my Miller Lite and shrugged. "Why deny it? That doesn't make me a wiseguy any more than taking on a job from you makes me a liberal."

He chuckled. "I didn't mean to suggest it did. It does seem . . . forgive me, Mr. Hammer. It does seem a trifle strange that a man who once made headlines killing mobsters would form an alliance with one."

"Alliance is too strong a word, Senator. I did a handful of jobs for him, unrelated to his . . . business. Matters he didn't want corrupted by his own associates."

"Could you be more specific?"

"No. Him dying doesn't mean client confidentiality goes out the window. That cop Hanson, in the other room, has the receipt for that C-note I signed before coming. Spells that out in the small print, if you're interested."

The dark eyebrows flicked up and down. "Actually, that's something of a relief. What I want to ask you dances along the edges of that confidentiality, Mr. Hammer. But I hope you might answer. And that you would trust me to be discreet as well."

"You can ask."

He folded his arms, like a big Irish genie about to grant a wish. "Did you receive something from the old don, shortly before . . . or perhaps *upon* . . . his death?"

"No. What would it have been if I had?"

"A book. A ledger, possibly."

I put the beer bottle back on the coffee table. "No. Is that what you're trying to recover? A ledger?"

He nodded. Now when he spoke it was nearly a whisper: "And here your discretion is key. The don was in power a very long time . . . going back to the late '40s. His ways, by modern standards, were old-fashioned, right up to the end. One particular antiquated practice peculiar to Don Giraldi was, apparently, keeping a handwritten record of every transaction, every agreement he ever made. No one knows precisely what was in that book . . . there were other books kept, accounting records that were largely fictional, intended for the IRS . . . but in this volume he was said to record the real events, the actual dealings of his business. When asked about such matters, he would say only, 'It's in the book.'"

I shrugged. "I heard the rumors. That he kept a book under lock and key or in a safe somewhere, and all his secrets were kept in the thing. But I never believed it."

"Why not?"

I pawed at the air dismissively. "He was too shrewd to write anything down. And incriminate himself if it fell into the wrong hands? Naw. It's a myth, Senator. If that's what you want to send me out looking for, my advice is forget it."

But the big head was shaking side to side. "No, Mr. Hammer, that book is very real. Old Nic told his most innermost associates, when his health began to fail earlier this year, that the book would be given to the person he trusted most."

I frowned, but I also shrugged. "So I'm wrong. Anyway, *I'm* not that person. He didn't send me the book. But how is it you know what his 'innermost associates' were told?"

"FBI wiretaps." His smile had a pixie-ish cast, but his eyes were so hard they might have been glass. "Do you think you could find that ledger, Mr. Hammer?"

I shrugged. "It's a big city. Puts the whole needle-in-a-haystack bit to shame. But what would you do with the thing? Does the FBI think they can make cases out of what's in those pages?"

He swallowed thickly. Suddenly he wasn't looking me in the eye. "There's no question, Mr. Hammer, that names and dates and facts and figures in a ledger would be of interest to law enforcement . . . both local and federal. There's also no question of its value to the old don's successors."

I was nodding. "Covering their own asses, and giving them valuable intel on the other mob families and crooked cops and any number of public figures. The blackmail possibilities alone are . . ."

But I didn't finish. Because the senator's head lowered and his eyes shut briefly, and I knew.

I knew.

"You've always been a straight shooter, Senator. But you didn't come from money. You must have needed help in the early days, getting started. You took money from the don, didn't you?"

"Mr. Hammer . . ."

"Hell. And so did somebody else." I hummed a few nasty off-key bars of "Hail to the Chief."

"Mr. Hammer, your country would be—"

"Can it. I put in my time in the Pacific. I should let you all swing. I should just sit back and laugh and laugh and let this play out like Watergate was just the cartoon before the main feature."

He looked very soft, this man who had come from such a hard place so long ago. "Is that what you intend to do?"

I sighed. Then I really did laugh, but there wasn't any humor in it. "No. I know what kind of foul waters you have to swim in, Senator. And your public record *is* good. Funny, the president having to send you—your politics couldn't be much more at odds. But you're stuck in the same mire, aren't you? Like dinosaurs in a tar pit."

That made him smile sadly. "Will you walk away and just let us decay, Mr. Hammer?"

"Why shouldn't I?"

"Well, for one thing, somewhere out there, in that big city, or that bigger country beyond, are people that Old Nic trusted. People like you, who aren't tainted by the Mob. And who are now in grave danger."

He was right about that.

"And Mr. Hammer, the way we came looking for you does not compare to the way other interested parties will conduct their search—the other five families, for example. And they may well start with you."

I grunted a laugh. "So I owe you a big thank you, at least, since I would have had no idea I was in anybody's crosshairs over this. I get that."

"Good. Good." He had his first overdue sip of beer. He licked foam off those rather sensual lips and the Leprechaun twinkle was back. "And what would you say to ten thousand dollars as a fee, Mr. Hammer?"

"Ten thousand dollars of the taxpayers' money?" I got up

and slapped on my hat. "Yeah. Why not? It's a way for me to get back some of what I paid in, anyway."

"Bring me the book, Mr. Hammer." His smile was reassuring but the eyes remained hard. "Bring *us* the book."

"See what I can do."

Hoods always come in twos. The bent-nose boys accompany their boss to business meetings, often in restaurants. Sometimes they sit with their boss, other times at an adjacent table. Or one sits nearby while the other stays outside in the car, at the wheel, an eye on the entrance. Or maybe parked in the alley behind a restaurant, which is a smarter move. Mob watchdogs are always teamed up in twos. So are assassins.

The guy waiting in the hall outside my office in the Hackard Building was in his twenties, wearing a yellow shirt with a pointy collar and no tie under a light-blue leisure suit that gave no hint of gun bulge. But a piece was under there, all right. He would have been handsome if his nose hadn't been broken into a misshapen thing, stuck on like clay a sculptor hadn't gotten around to shaping. His dark hair was puffy with hairspray and his sideburns were right off the cough-drop box.

Hoods these days.

"Let's go in and join your boss and your buddy," I said.

"What?" His voice was comically high-pitched and his eyes were small and stupid, all but disappearing when he frowned.

I made an educated guess. "You're with Sonny Giraldi's crew. And Sonny and your buddy are waiting inside. Inside my office. I'm Hammer." I jerked a thumb toward the door. "Like on the glass?"

He was still working that out when I went in, and held the door open for him.

John "Sonny" Giraldi, nephew of Don Nicholas Giraldi and assumed heir to the throne, was seated along the side wall like a patient waiting to get in to see the doctor. He was small, slender, olive-complected, with a narrow face, a hook nose, and big dark eyes that had a deceptively sleepy look. The other bodyguard, bigger than the guy in the hall, was another pointy-collared disco dude with heavy sideburns; he had a protruding forehead and a weak chin, sitting with a chair between himself and his boss.

Sonny's wardrobe, by the way, was likely courtesy of an Italian designer, Armani maybe, a sleekly cut gray number with a black shirt and gray silk tie. No way a gun was under there anywhere. Sonny let his employees handle the artillery, and the bad fashion statements.

"I'd prefer, Mr. Hammer," Sonny said, his voice a radio-announcer baritone too big for his small frame, "if you'd let Flavio keep his position in the corridor. This is a, uh . . . transitional time. I might attract unwanted company."

"Fine. Let Flavio stand watch. Hell, I know all about unwanted company."

That got a tiny twitch of a smile from Velda, over at her desk, but prior to that she had been sitting as blankly unconcerned as a meter maid making out a ticket. The Giraldi mob's heir apparent would not have suspected that the unseen right hand of this statuesque beauty undoubtedly held a revolver right now.

I shut the door on Flavio, giving him a sneer of a smile, and turned to walk toward my inner office door, saying, "Just you, Mr. Giraldi. I take it you're here for a consultation?"

He got to his feet—his Italian loafers had pointed toes—and gave me a nod that covered both questions, though he gave a flat-hand gesture to the seated bodyguard to stay that way. Velda's head swivelled slightly and I gave her a quick look that said be ready for anything. She returned that with a barely perceptible nod.

I shut the door and gestured Sonny Giraldi toward the client's chair. I got behind the desk as Sonny removed a silver cigarette case from inside his suitcoat. No chance he was going for a gun the way those threads fit. He reached his slender, well-manicured hand out to offer me a smoke from the case and I shook my head.

"I gave those up years ago," I said. "How do you think I managed to live so long?"

He smiled, a smile so delicious he seemed to taste it. "Well, a lot of us were wondering. Mr. Hammer, do you know why I'm here?"

"You want your uncle's ledger."

"Yes. Do you have it?"

"No. Next question."

He crossed his legs. He was not particularly manly, though not effeminate, either. "Do you understand why I thought you might have the book?"

"Yeah. On his deathbed, your uncle said he was bequeathing the thing to somebody he trusted."

He nodded slowly, the big dark sleepy eyes in the narrow face fixed on me. "You did a few jobs for the old don, jobs that he didn't feel he could entrust to his own people."

"That's true as far as it goes."

Now the big eyes narrowed to slits. "*Why* did he trust *you*, Mr. Hammer? And why would *you* work for *him*? You're well-known to be an enemy of La Cosa Nostra. Carl Evello. Alberto Bonetti. Two dons, representing two of the six families, and you killed them both. That massacre at the Y and S men's club, *how* many soldiers did you slaughter there, anyway? Thirty?"

"It was never proven I did that. Anyway, who's counting?"

Another tasty smile. There was an ashtray on my desk for the benefit of clients, and he used it, flicking ash with a hand heavy with bejeweled golden rings. The suit might be Armani, but down deep Sonny was still just another tacky goombah.

He was saying, "And yet Don Nicholas, Old Nic himself, not only let you live, he trusted you to do jobs for him. Why?"

"Why did he let me live? Now and then I killed his competitors. Which saved him trouble. As for why I would do a job for Old Nic . . . let's just say, he did me a favor now and then."

"What kind of favor, Mr. Hammer? Or may I call you 'Mike'—after all, you and my uncle were thick as thieves."

"Not that thick, but you can call me Mike . . . Sonny. Let's just say your uncle helped me out of the occasional jam in your world."

Oval eyes tightened to slits. "They say he helped you get out of town after the waterfront shootout with Sal Bonetti."

I said nothing.

Giraldi exhaled smoke, blowing it off to one side. Thoughtful of him.

"What is the government paying you?" he asked.

"What government? Paying me for what?"

"You were followed to the St. Moritz, Mike. Senator Boylan is staying there. The G wants the book—maybe to try to bring us down or maybe they got entries in there themself. I don't give two shits either way, Mike. I want that book."

"You've got an army. I'm just one guy. Go find it yourself."

Again he blew smoke to one side. His manner was casual but I could tell he was wound tight.

He said, "I have a feeling you're in a position to know where it is. Call it a hunch. But I don't think that book got sent to anybody in the family business. Because I was close to my uncle. *He would have given it to* me!"

He slammed a small fist onto my desk and the ashtray jumped. I didn't.

Very softly he repeated, "He would have given it to me."

I rocked back. "What use would somebody outside of the family have for that book?"

"I don't know. I honestly don't know, Mike."

"Does the thing even exist? Do you really believe that your uncle wrote down every important transaction and key business dealing in some ledger?"

He sat forward and the big eyes didn't seem at all sleepy now. "I *saw* him with it. The book exists. He would sit in his study—he wasn't a big man, he was my size, never one of these big fat slobs like so many in our business, a gray little guy always impeccably dressed, bald in his later years, and like . . . like a *monk* goin' over some ancient scroll he would, after anything big would go down, retire to his study and hunker over that goddamn book."

"What did it look like?"

"It was a ledger, but not a big one, not like an accountant uses. Smaller, more like an appointment book . . . but not *that* small. Maybe six by four. Beat-up looking brown cover, some kind of leather. But thick—three inches thick, anyway."

"Where did he keep it?"

"Well, it wasn't in his safe in that study. Or in a locked drawer, and we've been all over his house, looking." He sat forward and did his best to look earnest. "Mike, would it mean anything to you if I said the Giraldis are going to stay on the same path as Uncle Nic?"

"You mean prostitution, gambling, loan-sharking, that kind of thing? Am I supposed to be proud of you, Sonny?"

"You know that Uncle Nic never dealt drugs. We're the only one of the six families that stayed out of what he called an 'evil racket.' No kiddie porn, no underage hookers."

Did they give a Nobel Prize for conscientious racketeering, I wondered?

He was saying, too quickly, "And we—I—am gonna continue contributing to charities, through St. Pat's Old Cathedral in Little Italy. We fund orphanages and drug treatment centers and all kinds of good works, Mike. You know that. We're *alone* in that, of the six families."

"Okay. So you Giraldis are the best of the bad guys. What's that to me?"

He shrugged. "I suspect it's why you were willing to do jobs for my uncle. Not just because he bailed your ass out when crazy Sal Bonetti damn near killed you."

I trotted out my lopsided grin. "Sonny, I don't have the book."

"But you know where to look. There's one-hundred k in it for you, Mike, if you turn that book over to me. Cash."

"That's a lot of green for a ledger whose contents you aren't sure of."

"Find it, Mike. *Find* it."

Sonny got up, stubbed out his cigarette in the ashtray. Smoothed his suitcoat. "Do you think I'm the only one who knows that you were on the old boy's list of trusted associates? And do you think the other five families aren't going to be looking for that thing?"

Suddenly the government's ten thousand wasn't seeming like so much loot after all. Even Sonny's hundred k seemed short of generous.

"Of course, you can *handle* yourself, Mike. That's another reason why you're the ideal person to go looking for this particular volume. And any members of the other five families who you might happen to dispose of along the way, well, that's just a bonus for both of us."

He gave me a business card with his private numbers, with an after-hours one jotted on the back. Then he went out with a nod of goodbye that I didn't bother to return.

I just sat there thinking. I heard the door close in the outer office, and then Velda was coming in. She skirted the client's chair and leaned her palms on the desk. Her dark eyes were worried.

"What's going on, Mike? First cops, now wiseguys? What next?"

"I missed lunch," I said. "How about an early supper?"

She smirked and shook her head, making the arcs of raven-wing hair swing. "Only you would think of food at a time like this."

"Give Pat a call and have him meet us at the Blue Ribbon in half an hour."

"What makes you think a captain of Homicide is going to drop everything just because you call?"

"He'll drop everything because *you* called, doll. He has a thing for you, remember. And me? I'm the guy who solves half his cases."

The Blue Ribbon Restaurant on West Forty-fourth Street was in its between-lunch-and-supper lull, meaning Velda and I had the restaurant part of the bar damn near to ourselves. We sat

163

at our regular corner table with walls of autographed celebrity photos looking over our shoulders as I put away the knockwurst and Velda had a salad. She worked harder at maintaining her figure than I did.

Pushing her half-eaten rabbit food aside, Velda leaned in and asked, "So . . . you think you can find this ledger? What leads do you have?"

"Just two."

"Such as?"

I gulped from a pilsner of Miller. "Well, one is Father Mandano in Little Italy."

"Makes sense," she said with a nod. "His parish is where Don Giraldi was the primary patron."

I laughed shortly. "Patron. That's a good way to put it."

"Buying his way into heaven?"

"I don't think these mob guys really believe in God, not the top guys anyway. Buying himself good will is more like it. Like Capone in Chicago opening up soup kitchens in the Depression."

"So you'll talk to the good father."

"I will."

"That's one lead, Mike. You said two."

I looked at her slyly over the rim of my glass. I was almost whispering when I said, "Remember that job we did for Old Nic about twenty years back? That relocation number?"

Velda was nodding, smiling slyly right back at me. Like me, she kept her voice low. "You're right. That's a lead if ever there was one. You want me to come along?"

"I would. She liked you. She'll talk more freely if you're around. But I'll talk to the priest on my own."

"Yeah," she said with a smirk. "Only room for two in a confessional."

Pat came in the revolving door and came straight to us—he knew where we'd be. Enjoying the spring afternoon, he was in a lightweight tan suit, chocolate tie, and no hat—though he and I were two rare New Yorkers who still wore them. He stopped at the bar to grab a beer from George and brought it along with him when he came over, sitting with me on his left and Velda on his right.

"Don't wait for me," he said, noting the meal I was halfway through. "Dig right in."

"I said thirty minutes," I said. "You took forty-five. A man has to eat."

"Yeah, I heard that rumor. You didn't say what this was about, so let *me* tell *you*—old Don Giraldi finally croaking. Everybody and his dog is out looking for that legendary missing ledger of his."

"*Is* it legendary, Pat?"

His expression was friendly but the blue-gray eyes were hard. "Legendary in the sense that it's famous in certain circles. But I think it's very real, considering the stir it's causing among the lasagne set."

"The other families?"

"Just one, really—the Pierluigi bunch. They were the family that Old Nic was allied most closely with. Their territories really intertwined, you know. Talking to the OCU guys, they say Old Nic's reputation as the most beneficent of the Mafia capos is bullshit. Specifically, they say he invested in drug trafficking through Pierluigi. That and *other* nasty criminal enterprises that wouldn't have made the old don such a beloved figure around Little Italy."

"Meaning if the don really was keeping a record of his transactions," I said, "that book would be of high interest to the Pierluigi clan."

"Damn straight. But they aren't the only interested parties—there are a couple of underbosses in the Giraldi family who are looking at the old don's passing as an invitation to move up in the world."

"You mean, Sonny Giraldi doesn't have the don's chair sewn up."

"He might if he had that book. So, Mike." Pat's smile was wide but those eyes of his remained shrewd. "Do you have it?"

"Well, I may be older, but I hope I still have it. What would you say, Vel? Do I still have it?"

"I should say you do," she said.

"Can the comedy," Pat said. "It's well-known you had a soft spot for Old Nic, Mike."

"That's horseshit, Pat. I had no illusions about the old boy. He was probably the best man in his world, but what a lousy world, huh?"

Pat sipped beer, then almost whispered: "Word on the street is, that book went to somebody the old don trusted. Are *you* that somebody, Mike?"

"No. Tell me about this guy Hanson."

"Hanson? *What* Hanson?"

"Hanson on the department. He didn't show me his badge but he didn't have to. He had a buddy with him whose name I didn't catch—younger guy."

"That would likely be Captain Bradley."

I grinned at him. "Captain! How about that? A young guy achieving such a rarefied rank. You must be impressed, Pat."

"Screw you, buddy. Hanson is an ass-kisser . . . my apologies, Velda . . . and a political player from way back. He made inspector at thirty-five. You never ran into him before?"

"No."

"When *did* you run into him?"

I ignored the question. "So this Hanson is strictly a One Police Plaza guy? No wonder I don't know him. But is he honest?"

"Define honest."

"Is he *bent*, Pat? Not just a little, but all the way?"

Pat shook his head. "I don't think so."

"You don't sound very convinced."

"We don't travel in the same orbit, Hanson and me. Mike, I never heard a whisper of corruption in regard to him, but that doesn't make it impossible. I mean, he's a political animal."

I gave him a small, nasty smile. "Could Inspector Hanson be in that ledger?"

Pat had a sip of beer and thought about it. "If he *is* bent, of course he could. But so could any number of bad apples. Why, did he come looking for it?"

I ignored that question, too. "Seems to me there are a lot of people with guns who might like to check this book out of whoever's library it's landed in."

"Brother, you aren't kidding."

I put a hand on his shoulder. "Pat, let me treat you to a platter of this knockwurst. On me."

"What's the occasion for such generosity?"

"I just think it's a pity that average citizens like me don't take the time out, now and again, to properly thank a public servant like you for your stalwart efforts."

"Stalwart, huh? Normally I'd say 'baloney.'"

But instead he ordered the knockwurst.

St. Patrick's Cathedral on Fifth Avenue, built in the 1870s, was a late arrival compared to old St. Pat's on the corner of Prince and Mott. The first St. Pat's had started saving souls in Little Italy a good seventy years before that.

I sat with Father Mandano in his office in the Prince Street rectory—this was a Wednesday night with no mass at old St. Pat's. Velda sat outside in the reception area, reading an ancient issue of *Catholic Digest*—a desk where her nun equivalent usually sat was empty. This was early evening, after office hours.

The broad-shouldered priest, in casual black and that touch of white, sat with thick-fingered, prayerfully folded hands on the blotter of a massive contradiction of a desk, its austere lines trimmed with ornamental flourishes. The office with its rich wood paneling and arched windows had a conference table to one side and bookcases everywhere, the generous, burnished chamber under-lit by way of a banker's lamp and a few glowing wall-mounted fixtures, the desk itself cluttered with work.

The father was as legendary in Little Italy as that ledger of Don Giraldi's—the old priest deemed tough but fair, his generosity renowned. Still, even in his seventies, he had the well-fed look and hard eyes of a line coach, his white hair cut military short, his square head home to regular features that were distorting with age.

"I have of course heard the tales about this notorious ledger, Michael," he said in a sonorous baritone schooled for the pulpit. "But the late don did not leave it with me."

"You had many meetings with Giraldi over the years, Father. Would you have any notion about who he might have entrusted with that book?"

He shook his head once, a solemn and final gesture. "I only met rarely with Mr. Giraldi. For many years, I dealt solely with his wife, Antonietta, who was a wonderful, devout woman."

"How could she be devout and married to a mob boss?"

"Our Father's house has many mansions."

"Yeah, and compartments, too, I guess. And mob money can build plenty of mansions."

His smile was barely perceptible. "When were you last at mass, Michael? I assume you are of the faith, Irish lad that you are."

"I haven't been a 'lad' for a lot of years, Father, and I haven't been to mass since I got back from overseas."

"The war changed you."

"The war showed me that God either doesn't give a damn or has some sick sense of humor. If you'll forgive my frankness, Father."

The dark eyes didn't look so hard now. "I'm in the forgiveness business, Michael. You hold God responsible for the sins of man?"

"If you mean war, Father, fighting against an evil devil like Hitler isn't considered a sin, is it?"

"No. But I would caution you that holding God responsible for the actions of men is a dangerous philosophy. And I gather, from your words, that you *do* believe in God."

"I do."

There was nothing barely perceptible about his smile now. "Years ago, the headlines were filled with your colorful activities, working against evil men. You were raised in the church, so surely you know of St. Michael."

"Yeah, the avenging archangel."

"Well, that's perhaps an oversimplification. Among other things, he leads the army of God against the minions of Satan, the powers of Hell."

"I'm semi-retired from that, Father. Let's just say you don't have time to hear *my* confession. But I bet you heard some beauts from Old Nic."

The smile disappeared and the priest's countenance was solemn again. "Nicholas Giraldi never came to confession. Not once."

"What?"

"Oh, he will lie in consecrated ground. I gave him bedside Last Rites at St. Luke's. But he never took confession. And I will confess to you, Michael, that I was surprised when, after his wife's death, he continued to fund her charities. If there was any purpose in it, other than his own self-aggrandizement, it might have been to honor her memory."

"He bought himself a lot of good will here in Little Italy."

"He did. But I don't believe his good works had anything to do with seeking forgiveness. And before you ask how I could accept contributions from the likes of Don Giraldi, I will tell you that even a spiritual man, a servant of God, must live in the physical world. If suffering can be alleviated by accepting such contributions, I will accept that penance, whether sincere or cynical. You might consider this in itself a cynical, even selfish practice, Michael. But we were put here in this place, this, this . . ."

"Vale of tears, Father?"

"Vale of tears, son. We were put here in this problem-solving world, this physical purgatory, to exercise our free will. And if I can turn ill-gotten gains into the work of the Lord, I will do so, unashamed."

Why shouldn't he? All he had to do was take confession from some other collar, and get his sins washed away for a few Hail Marys. But I didn't say that. Hypocritical or not, Father Mandano had helped a lot of people. He was a practical man and that wasn't a sin in my book.

I got to my feet, my hat in my hands. "Thanks for seeing me at short notice, Father. Listen, if you happen to get a line on that ledger, let me know. It could spark a shooting war out on your streets. And innocent people could die."

"And that troubles you, doesn't it, Michael?"

"Don't kid yourself, Father. This is just a job to me. I have a big payday coming if I pull this off. This is one valuable book."

"In my line of work, Michael," he said, "there is only *one* book of real value."

Wilcox in Suffolk County was a prosperous-looking little beach burg with a single industry: tourism. In a month the population would swell from seven thousand to who-the-hell-knew, and the business district would be alive and jumping till all hours. Right now, at eight-thirty p.m., it was a ghost town.

Sheila Burrows lived in a two-bedroom brick bungalow on a side street, perched on a small but nicely landscaped yard against a wooded backdrop. The place was probably built in the fifties, nothing fancy but well-maintained. A freestanding matching brick one-car garage was just behind the house. We pulled in up front. The light was on over the front door. We were expected.

I got out of the car and came around to play gentleman for Velda, but she was already climbing out. She had changed into a black pantsuit and a gray silk blouse and looked very businesslike, or as much as her curves, long legs and all that shoulders-brushing raven hair allowed. She carried a good-size black purse with a shoulder strap. Plenty of room for the various female accoutrements, including a .22 revolver.

She was looking back the way we came. "I can't shake the feeling we were followed," she said.

"Hard to tell on a damn expressway," I admitted. "But I didn't pick up on anything on that county road."

"Maybe I should stay out here and keep watch."

"No. I can use you inside. I remember you hitting it off with this broad. She was scared of me, as I recall."

Now Velda was looking at the brick house. "Well, for all she knew you were one of Don Giraldi's thugs and she was getting a one-way ride. And maybe something about your manner said that a 'broad' is what you thought she was."

"I wasn't so cultured then."

"Yeah," she said sarcastically, as we started up the walk. "You've come a long way, baby."

Twenty years ago, more or less, Velda and I had moved Sheila Burrows out to these Long Island hinterlands. That hadn't been her name then, and she'd had to leave a Park Avenue penthouse to make the move. The exact circumstances as to why Don Giraldi had wanted his mistress to disappear had not been made known to us. But we had suspected.

The woman who met us at the door was barely recognizable as the former Broadway chorus girl we had helped relocate back when LBJ was still president. She had been petite and curvy and platinum blonde. She was now stout and bulgy and mousy brunette. Her pretty Connie Stevens-ish features, lightly made up, were trapped inside a round ball of a face.

"Nice to see you two again," she said as she ushered us inside. She wore a pink top, blue jeans and sandals.

There was no entryway. You were just suddenly in the living room, a formal area with lots of plastic-covered furniture. A spinet piano against the left wall was overseen by a big gilt-framed pastel portrait of our hostess back in all her busty, blonde glory.

She quickly moved us into a small family room area just off a smallish kitchen with wooden cabinets and up-to-date appliances; a short hallway to bedrooms was at the rear. She sat us down at a round maple table with captain's chairs and a spring-themed centerpiece of plastic flowers.

She had coffee ready for us. As I stirred milk and sugar into mine, I glanced at the nearby wall where gray-washed wooden paneling was arrayed with framed pictures. They charted two things: her descent into near obesity, and the birth, adolescence and young manhood of a son. It was all there, from playpen to playground, from high school musical to basketball court, from graduation to what was obviously a recent shot of the handsome young man with an attractive girl outside a building I recognized as part of NYU.

"That's our son," she said, in a breathy second soprano that had been sexy once upon a time.

"We *thought* you were pregnant," Velda said with a tiny smile.

Her light blue eyes jumped. "Really? You knew? Why, I was only a few months gone. Barely showing."

"You just had that glow," Velda said.

Our hostess chuckled. "More likely water retention. How *do* you maintain that lovely figure of yours, Miss Sterling? Or are you two *married* by now?"

"Not married," Velda said. "Not quite. Not yet."

"She eats a lot of salad," I said.

That made Sheila Burrows wince, and Velda shot me a look. I'd been rude. Hadn't meant to be, but some things come naturally.

I said, "You probably never figured to see us again."

"That's true," she said. She sipped her coffee. "But I wasn't surprised to hear from you, not exactly."

Velda asked, "Why is that?"

"With Nicholas dying, I figured there would be *some* kind of follow-up. For a long time, there was a lawyer, a nice man named Bradley, who handled the financial arrangements. He would come by every six months and see how I was doing. And ask questions about our son."

I asked, "Any direct contact with Don Giraldi since you moved out here?"

"No. And, at first, I was surprised. I thought after Nick was born . . . our son is Nicholas, too . . . that we might, in some way, resume our relationship. Nicolas Giraldi was a very charming man, Mr. Hammer. Very suave. Very courtly. He was the love of my life."

"You were only with him for, what? Five or six years?"

"Yes, but it was a wonderful time. We traveled together, even went to Europe once, and he practically lived with me, during those years. I don't believe he ever had relations with his wife after the early years of their marriage."

"They had three daughters."

"Yes," she said, rather defensively, "but none after our Nick came along."

Funny that she so insistently referred to the son in that fashion—"our Nick"—when the father had avoided any direct contact. And this once beautiful woman, so sexually desirable on and off the stage, had become a homemaker and mother—a suburban housewife. Without a husband.

Velda said, "I can see why you thought Nicholas would come back to you, after your son's birth. If he had really wanted you out of his life . . . for whatever reason . . . he wouldn't have kept you so close to home."

"Wilcox is a long way from Broadway," she said rather wistfully.

"But it's not the moon," I said. "I had assumed the don

felt you'd gotten too close to him—that you'd seen things that could be used against him."

Her eyes jumped again. "Oh, I would never—"

"Not by you, but by others. Police. FBI. Business rivals. But it's clear he wanted his son protected. So that the boy would not be used against him."

She was nodding. "That's right. That's what he told me, before he sent me away. He said our son would be in harm's way, if anyone knew he existed. But that he would *always* look out for young Nick. That someday Nick would have a great future."

Velda said, "You said you had no direct contact with Nicholas. But would I be right in saying that you had . . . *indirect* contact?"

The pretty face in the plump setting beamed with pride. "Oh yes. Maybe once a year, always in a different way. Nick is a very talented boy, talented young *man* now. He took part in so many school activities, both the arts and sports. And *so* brilliant, valedictorian of his class! But then his father was a genius, wasn't he?"

I asked, "What do you mean, 'once a year, always in a different way?'"

She was looking past me at the wall of pictures. Fingers that were still slender, graceful, traced a memory in the air.

"There Nicholas would be," she said, "in the audience at a concert, or a ball game, or a school play . . . I think Nick gets his artistic talent from me, if that doesn't sound too stuck up . . . and best of all, Nicholas came to graduation, and heard his son speak."

Velda asked, "Did they ever meet?"

"No." She pointed past Velda. "Did you notice that picture? That one high up, at the left?"

A solemn portrait of a kid in army green preceded the first of several baby photos.

"That's a young man who died in Vietnam," she said. "Mr. Bradley, the attorney, provided me with that and other photos, as well as documents. His name was Edwin Burrows and we never met. He was an only child with no immediate family. He won several medals, actually, including a Silver Star, and *that* was the father that Nick grew up proud of."

I asked, "No suspicions?"

"Why should he be suspicious? When he was younger, Nick was very proud of his heroic father."

"Only when he was younger?"

"Well . . . you know boys. They grow out of these things."

Not really, but I let it pass.

"Mrs. Burrows," I said, sitting forward, "have you received anything, perhaps in the mail, that might seem to have come from Don Giraldi?"

"No . . ."

"Specifically, a ledger. A book."

Her eyes were guileless. "No," she said. "No. After Mr. Bradley died, and his visits ended, another lawyer came around, just once. I was given a generous amount of money and told I was now on my own. And there's a trust fund for Nick that becomes his on his graduation from NYU."

"Have you talked to your son recently?"

She nodded. "We talk on the phone at least once a week. Why, I spoke to him just yesterday."

"Did he say anything about receiving a ledger from his father?"

"Mr. Hammer, no. As I thought I made clear, as far as Nick

is concerned *his* father is a Vietnam war hero named Edwin Burrows."

"Right," I said. "Now listen carefully."

And I told her about the book.

She might be a suburban hausfrau now, but she had once been the mistress of a mob boss. She followed me easily, occasionally nodding, never interrupting.

"You are on the very short list," I said, "of people who Don Giraldi valued and trusted. You might *still* receive that book. And it's possible some very bad people might come looking for it."

She shook her head, mousy brown curls bouncing. "Doesn't seem possible . . . after all these years. I thought I was safe . . . I thought *Nick* was safe."

"You raise the most pertinent point. I think your son is the logical person the don may have sent that book."

She frowned in concern, but said nothing.

I went on: "I want you to do two things, Mrs. Burrows, and I don't want any argument. I want you to let us stow you away in a safe-house motel we use upstate. Until this is over. You have a car? Velda will drive you in it, and stay with you till I give the word. Just quickly pack a bag."

She swallowed and nodded. "And the other thing?"

"I want you to call your son right now," I said, "and tell him I'm coming to visit him. I'll talk to him briefly myself, so that he'll know my voice. I'll come alone. If more than one person shows up at his door, even if one of them claims to be me, he's not to let them in. If that happens, he's to get out and get away, as fast as he can. Is all of that clear?"

She wore a funny little smile. "You know, Mr. Hammer,

I think my impression of you all those years ago was wrong, very wrong."

"Yeah?"

"You really are quite a nice, caring human being."

I glanced at Velda, who wasn't bothering to stifle her grin.

"Yeah," I said. "I get that a lot."

If Wilcox at eight-thirty p.m. was a ghost town, the East Village at eleven-something was a freak show. This was a landscape of crumbling buildings, with as many people living on the streets as walking down them, where in a candy store you could buy a Snickers Bar or an eightball of smack, and when morning came, bodies with bullet holes or smaller but just as deadly ones would be on sidewalks and alleyways like so much trash set out for collection.

Tompkins Square Park was this neighborhood's central gathering place, from oldtimers who had voted for FDR and operated traditional businesses like diners and laundries to students, punkers, artists, and poets seeking life experience and cheap lodging. Every second tenement storefront seemed to be home to a gallery showcasing work inspired by the tragic but colorful street life around them. NYU student Nick Burrows lived in a second-floor apartment over a gallery peddling works by an artist whose canvases of graffiti struck me as little different from the free stuff on alley walls.

His buzzer worked, which was saying something in this neighborhood, and he met me on a landing as spongy as the steps coming up had been. He wore a black CBGB T-shirt, jeans and sneakers, a kid of twenty-two with the wiry frame of his father but taller, and the pleasant features of his mother, their prettiness turned masculine by heavy eyebrows.

He offered his hand and we shook under the dim yellowish glow of a single mounted bulb. "I appreciate you helping out my mom, Mr. Hammer. You know, I think I've heard of you."

"A lot of people think they've heard of me," I said, moving past him into the apartment. "They're just not sure anymore."

His was a typical college kid's pad—thrift-shop furnishings, atomic-age stuff that had looked modern in the fifties and seemed quaint now. Plank and cement-block bookcases lined the walls, paperbacks and school books mostly, and the occasional poster advertising an East Village art show or theatrical production was taped here and there to the brick walls. The kitchenette area was off to one side and a doorless door led to a bedroom with a waterbed. We sat on a thin-cushioned couch with sparkly turquoise upholstery.

He offered me a smoke and I declined. He had one as he leaned back, an arm along the upper cushions, and studied me like the smart college kid he was. His mother had told him on the phone that I had something important to talk to him about, and his need for caution. I had spoken to him briefly, as well, but nothing about the book.

Still, he'd been told there was danger and he seemed unruffled. There was strength in this kid.

I said, "You know who your real father was, don't you, Nick?"

He nodded.

I grinned. "I figured a smart kid like you would do some poking into that Vietnam-hero malarkey. Did the don ever get in touch with you? He came to the occasional school event, I understand."

The young man shook his head. "Get in touch? No, not in the sense that he ever introduced himself. But he began seeking me out after a concert, a basketball game, just to come up and say, 'Good job tonight,' or 'Nice going out there.' Shook my hand a couple of times."

"So you noticed him."

"Yeah, and when I got older, I recognized him. He was in the papers now and then, you know. I did some digging on my own, old newspaper files and that kind of thing. Saw my mom's picture, too, back when she was a real knockout. She wasn't just a chorus girl, you know, like the press would have it. She had speaking parts, got mentioned in reviews, sometimes."

"Your mother doesn't know that you know any of this."

"Why worry her?"

"Nick, I'm here because your father kept a ledger, a book said to contain all of his secrets. Word was he planned to give it to the person he trusted most in the world. Are you that person?"

He sighed, smiled, allowed himself a private laugh.

Then he asked, "Would you like a beer? You look like a guy who could use a beer."

"Has been a long day."

So he got us cold cans of beer and he leaned back and I did too. And he told me his story.

Two weeks ago, he'd received a phone call from Don Nicholas Giraldi—a breathy voice that had a deathbed ring to it, and a request that young Nick come to a certain hospital room at St. Luke's. No mention of old Nicholas being young Nick's father, not on the phone.

"But when I stood at his bedside," Nick said, "he told me. He said, 'I'm your father.' Very melodramatic. Ever see 'Star Wars'? 'Luke, I am your father'? Like that."

"And what did you say?"

He shrugged. "Just, 'I know. I've known for years.' That seemed to throw the old boy, but he didn't have the wind or the energy to discuss it or ask for details or anything. He just said, 'You're going to come into money when you graduate from the university.'"

"You didn't know there was a trust fund?"

"No. And I still don't know how much is in it. I'll be happy to accept whatever-it-is, because I think I kind of deserve it, growing up without a father. I'm hoping it'll be enough for me to start a business. Don't let the arty neighborhood fool you, Mr. Hammer—I'm a business major."

"Is that what Old Nic had in mind, you starting up something of your own?"

The young man frowned, shook his head. "I'm not sure. He may have wanted me to step into *his* role in his . . . his organization. Or he may have been fine with me going my own way. In any event, he said, 'I have something for you. Whatever you do in life, it will be valuable to you.'"

"The book?"

He nodded. "The book, Mr. Hammer. The book of my father's secrets."

I sat forward. "Containing everything he knew, a record of every crooked thing he'd done, and all of those he'd conspired with to break God knows how many laws." I shook my head. "Even if you go down a straight path, son, that book would be valuable."

He nodded. "It's valuable, all right. But I don't want it, Mr. Hammer. I'm not interested in it or what it represents."

"What are you going to do with the thing?"

"Give it to you." He shrugged. "Do what you will with it. I want only one thing in return."

"Yeah?"

"Ensure that my mother is safe. That she is not in any danger. And do the same for me, if you can. But Mom . . . she did so much for me, sacrificed everything, gave her *life* to me . . . I want her *safe*."

"I think I can handle that."

He extended his hand for me to shake, and I did.

He got up and went over to a plank-and-block bookcase under the window onto the neon-winking street. I followed him. He was selecting an ancient-looking sheepskin-covered volume from a stack of books carelessly piled on top when the door splintered open, kicked in viciously, and two men burst in with guns in hand.

First in was Flavio, still wearing the light-blue suit and yellow pointy-collar shirt, but I never did get the name of his pal, the big guy with the weak chin and Neanderthal forehead. They come in twos, you know, hoods who work for guys like Sonny Giraldi.

They had big pieces in their fists, matching .357 mags. In this part of town, where gunshots were commonplace, who needed .22 autos with silencers? The big guy fell back to be framed in the doorway like another work of East Village art, and Flavio took two more steps inside, training his .357 on both of us, as young Nick and I were clustered together.

Hoods always came in twos.

Flavio, in his comically high-pitched voice, said, "Is that the book? Give me that goddamned *book*!"

"Take it," Nick said, frowning, more disgusted than afraid, and he stepped forward, holding out the small, thick volume, blocking me as he did.

I used that to whip the .45 from under my shoulder, and I shoved the kid to the floor and rode him down, firing up.

Flavio may have had a .357, but that's a card a .45 trumps easy, particularly if you get the first shot off, and even more so if you make it a head shot that cuts off any motor action. What few brains the bastard had got splashed in a shower of bone and blood onto his startled pal's puss, and the Neanderthal reacted like he'd been hit with a gory pie, giving me the half second I needed to shatter that protruding forehead with a slug and paint an abstract picture on the brick out in that landing, worthy of any East Village gallery.

Now Nick was scared, taking in the bloody mess on his doorstep. "Jesus, man! What are you going to do?"

"Call a cop. You got a phone?"

"Yeah, yeah, call the cops!" He was pointing. "Phone's over there."

I picked the sheepskin-covered book up off the floor. "No—not the cops. *A* cop."

And I called Pat Chambers.

I didn't call Sonny Giraldi until I got back to the office around three a.m. I had wanted to get that valuable book into my office safe.

The heir to the old don's throne pretended I'd woken him, but I knew damn well he'd been up waiting to hear from his boys. Or maybe some cop in his pocket had already called to say the apartment invasion in the East Village had failed, in which case it was unlikely Sonny would be in the midst of a soothing night's sleep when I used the private number he'd provided me.

Cheerfully I asked, "Did you know that your boy Flavio and his slopehead buddy won a free ride to the county morgue tonight?"

"What?"

"I sent them there. Just like you sent them to the Burrows kid's apartment. They'd been following me, hadn't they? I really *must* be getting old. Velda caught it, but I didn't."

The radio-announcer voice conveyed words in a tumble. "Hammer, I didn't send them. They must be working for one of my rivals or something. I played it absolutely straight with you, I swear to God."

"No you didn't. You wanted me to lead you to the book, and whoever had it needed to die, because they knew what was in it, and I had to die, just to keep things tidy. Right? Who would miss an old broken-down PI like me, anyway?"

"Believe me, Hammer, I—"

"I don't believe you, Sonny. But you can believe me."

Actually, I was about to tell him a whopper, but he'd never know.

I went on: "This book will go in a safe deposit box in some distant bank, and will not come out again until my death. If that death is nice and peaceful, I will leave instructions that the book be burned. If I have an unpleasant going away party, then that book will go to the feds. Understood?"

". . . Understood."

"And the Burrows woman and her son, they're out of this. Any harm befalls either one, that book comes out of mothballs and into federal hands. *Capeesh?*"

"*Capeesh,*" he said glumly.

"Then there's the matter of my fee."

"Your *fee!* What the hell—"

"Sonny, I found the book for you. You owe me one hundred grand."

His voice turned thin and nasty. "I heard a lot of bad things about you, Hammer. But I never heard you were a blackmailing prick."

"Well, you learn something every day, if you're paying attention. I want that hundred k donated to whatever charities that Father Mandano directs. Think of the fine reputation you'll earn, Sonny, continuing your late uncle's good works in Little Italy."

And I hung up on him.

Cops always come in twos, they say, but the next morning, when Hanson entered my private office, he left his nameless crony in the outer one to read old magazines and enjoy the view of Velda, back at her reception desk.

"Have a seat, Inspector," I said, getting behind my desk.

The brown sheepskin volume, its spine ancient and cracked, lay on my blotter at a casual angle, where I'd tossed it in anticipation of his visit.

"*That's* the book," he said, eyes wide.

"That's the book. And it's all yours for ten grand."

"May I?" he asked, reaching for it.

"Be my guest."

He thumbed it open. Pleasure turned to confusion on his face, then to shock.

"My God . . ." he said.

"It's valuable, all right. I'm no expert, though, so you might have overpaid. You may want to hold onto it for a while."

"I'll be damned," he said, leafing through.

"As advertised, it has in it everything the old don knew about dirty schemes and double-dealing. Stuff that applies to crooks and cops and senators and even presidents."

He was shaking his head, eyes still on the book.

"Of course, we *were* wrong about it being a ledger. It's more a how-to-book by another Italian gangster. First-edition English-language translation, though—1640, it says."

"A gangster named Machiavelli," Hanson said dryly.

"And a book," I said, "called *The Prince*."

SKIN

If it weren't for the hand lying next to the carnage wreaked on a human body, you would have thought it was road kill that half a dozen vehicles had rolled over.

This was something out of a war zone, not what you expected to find just off the highway in rural upstate New York. A glistening string of tendon seeped into splintered bone, a grisly signpost that this had been a body, a living, viable human animal. Now it was barely identifiable as something that used to think and talk. Unless that lonely hand's fingerprints had something to say.

Pat Chambers, Captain of Homicide back in the city, gave me one of those long, steady stares I had been on the receiving end of for decades. He was a big guy, like me, his suit less rumpled than mine, and we were rare holdouts who still stuck hats on our aging skulls.

"How'd you find this, Mike?"

I had to shrug. "Sure as hell wasn't looking for it. Something caught my eye, driving by."

This was a late September afternoon and cool. A low hanging sun ricocheted off the dying trees of the nearby woods. We were on our way back from an event at the Police Academy and had taken separate cars but I'd wanted to get there early and talk to an instructor who was about to retire. We were cadets together. A long time ago.

"Great. Just swell." Pat kept staring at me, those gray-blue eyes barely blinking. "The bushes here cover that mess up pretty well. From a moving car going in either direction, it's damn near invisible. And yet it caught your eye?"

I shook my head. "I didn't make that thing from the highway." I pointed near the roadside. "There was a dog there, stretched out pointer fashion, and shivering like it had tripped over a puma. Had its teeth bared, and I sure knew something was up."

"And that was enough to make you stop your car."

"Hey, I still got reflexes in my old age! I jammed on my brakes, pulled over and got out."

That smile of his was damn near a sneer. "What if it *had* been a puma?"

I patted under my arm where the holstered .45 lived.

"Anyway," I said, and shrugged, "the mutt took its eyes away, spotted me and ran. If it *had* been a puma, Rover would have just backed off slowly."

He sighed. "So you had a look."

"Right."

"And now we're in the middle of this and won't get back for hours."

"So I'm a good citizen."

He nodded toward the mess. "And what did you think when you saw . . . that?"

"Figured somebody fell out of a plane."

"You still think so?"

I let out a grunt and shook my head. "Couldn't have been. A body would have splashed. Would've come in at an angle and likely got torn up by those trees."

"Maybe that's what's left of an animal's supper."

I shook my head. "A predator wouldn't dine roadside. And if it made its attack in the woods, over there, this mess would've stayed there. Anyway, no animal did this."

"You sound sure."

"Well, a human animal maybe. But not anything that lives in those woods."

"Yeah? Why?"

I showed him my teeth. "Too much meat left." I shook my head again. "This body was dumped here."

Pat took a step closer and inspected the ball of entrails, then stepped back. "Somebody carry it in his arms, you think?"

"Like a bride over the threshold? That would have been messy. Imagine what would get on your clothes. Of course, the thing might have been wrapped up in plastic. Or maybe the killer used a big shopping bag. Or butcher paper."

"You're talking killer already?"

"Somebody dead got dumped. That spells killer."

Pat didn't argue, eyes searching the area. "You're probably right that this body was conveyed somehow. No drag marks."

"Real professional."

"How about magical," Pat muttered. "I *knew* we should have come up here in one car. You just cannot be left to your own devices. No, instead you have to leave first, and I have to stop like a good goddamn Samaritan because I think you have a flat or something."

I showed him a small grin. "You couldn't abandon me out in the sticks, buddy, and get a good night's sleep."

"I'll get a good night's sleep after viewing this mess of meat?"

I laughed at him. "Hey, at least no local cop is going to be hauling me over the coals. You have a badge to back me up with an alibi."

He growled sarcastically, "Oh, you're so famous they know you outside New York City, I suppose?"

"Oh yeah," I said, "they know me. They have television up here and everything." Then I let out a little chuckle. "They may even have heard of you. How about that?"

"Yeah, how about that." His tone was sour.

I put my hand on his shoulder. "Lighten up, Pat. Didn't you like my pep talk to those rookies? Hell, didn't I play you up, bigtime?"

He smirked. "Yeah, thanks. Your talk of an 'impending much-overdue promotion' can rattle a few cages up the food chain, pal. It's bad enough even being mentioned in the same breath with you."

"So they've heard of me, up the food chain, then? You know, I mostly been staying out of trouble in my golden years."

I moved in for a closer look at the scarlet and splintered white and stringy mess with slithery things weaving them together and unidentifiable strips of hair and gristle poking out of impossible places.

You used to be somebody, I thought.

Hell, so did I.

I said, "You'd better quit pouting and call in the troops, buddy. The local newspaper will pick up the call, too, most likely. And having a police photog out here fast won't do a bit of harm either."

Under his breath Pat said something unintelligible. While he got out his cell and made the call, the thought of photos sent me to my car, where I got the digital camera and grabbed a dozen color shots of the mangled pile of human body parts and the area around it. I put the camera back and waited there with Pat for the locals to show.

It took hardly any time for the black-and-white to roll up to us. Two guys got out, both in uniform, a heavyset middle-aged sergeant and a skinny young patrolman.

Pat flashed his NYPD badge and the sergeant nodded politely and said, "Captain." He held out his hand and Pat took it.

"Mal Tooney," the older cop said. "We were right up the road when the call came in. The other crew should be here in a few minutes. Where's the body?"

Pat indicated the direction with a nod and the sergeant and his young driver followed him into the brush. I tagged after. We didn't have to go in very far at all. The well-seasoned sergeant took in a deep breath and swallowed. His young partner just puked.

"Ever see anything like that before?" I asked the older cop, keeping the grin down.

"Not like that," Sergeant Tooney said. "You?"

"A couple of times," I told him. Then explained, "A few wars ago."

"I've seen some car crash victims pretty tore up," he said, and took off his cap and brushed back what hair he had left. "But this? Damn."

The patrolman was still puking. Lot in his stomach, for a skinny kid. Finally, sheepishly, he wiped his mouth and turned his head away. "I'm new at this," he admitted.

"You'll get used to it," Pat told him.

Used to frequent death and everyday gore, maybe. But getting used to running across something this ghastly? Not bloody likely, as the Brits say.

Both of us gave an initial report to the sergeant while the rookie jotted it down in detail. Just as we finished, another squad car drove up with a white station wagon tagging behind.

The call letters of a television station were emblazoned on the doors and a young guy in jeans and a sweatshirt with the same call letters jumped out of the passenger side with a shoulder-mounted TV camera that sat there like a robotic second head.

The driver got out slowly, one of those impossible beauties who seem to have taken over the bright spots on the networks, and if looks and style were anything, this tall lovely brunette in a tight blue jumpsuit was well on her way to the big studios in Manhattan.

I grinned at Pat. "Looks like we're going to make the evening news on this one."

Pat put out an arm and held me back, getting me out of the way. Seemed the young cameraman was real eager. He was moving fast, an eye glued to the viewfinder, as he rushed in for the shot, took his eye away for one second while he scoped the terrible sight in front of him, then vomited all over himself.

He gave a pathetic little look around him, and, out of sheer desperation, triggered the camera and tilted forward to capture the whole scene in glaring color.

Pat and I exchanged looks as the sick smell wafted its way to us. We both knew no TV station manager would allow that kind of thing to go on the air, not without pixelating it beyond recognition.

Maybe it would find its way to the Internet for all the horror lovers out there.

The lovely newscaster came over to us and introduced herself. Her skin had an ivory glow in an afternoon giving way to dusk.

SHIN

"Melodie Anderson, Eye Witness News. Why, you're Mike Hammer!"

I gave Pat a nasty little sideways grin and he smirked and shook his head.

"In the flesh," I said.

Her smile was flirtatious. "You don't look a day over fifty."

At my age, that was a compliment. But she was immediately embarrassed, thinking she'd insulted me.

"Sorry," she said. "My late father was in the news business, too. He covered a lot of your stories, years ago. He thought you were a great guy."

Pat said, "That's because Mr. Hammer here used to generate a lot of news."

Her eyes were a lovely light hazel. "And you're Pat Chambers! Captain Chambers."

Now it was Pat's turn to give me a self-satisfied look.

I said, "If what you're saying is that I'm old enough to be your father, doll, I plead guilty."

The "doll" amused her. "Is that right?"

"That's right. That's the bad news. The good news is, I'm *not* your father."

That made her laugh and Pat shook his head, muttering something to the effect that I would never change.

Her gaze hopped from me to Pat and back again. "Are you gentlemen willing to be interviewed on camera?"

I said yes and Pat said no, but finally he came around, qualifying it, "No speculation on what this is or what might have happened here. Just the facts."

"Like *Dragnet*," I said.

"Used to watch that show on TVLand," she said, "when I was a kid."

Ouch.

So she interviewed us, and we kept it factual, and afterward the locals wanted to talk to Pat, and the brunette newscaster took me gently by the arm and walked me away a ways.

"It's just a coincidence," she said, "Mike Hammer coming on to what might be a murder scene?"

"Just a coincidence. Now, if I were coming on to you, that would be premeditated."

"Would you be surprised if I said I had a thing for older men?"

"More like relieved. But, doll, I'm taken. Engaged."

"Long engagement?"

"When were you born?"

She told me.

I said, "Before that."

That made her blink, then she smiled again. "I don't want to date you, Mr. Hammer. Or if I do, I'll respect your . . . long engagement. But I do want to know what you think happened here."

"Off the record?"

"Off the record, if that's all I can get."

"Honey, I don't have a clue. Let the high-tech boys have a swing at that mess over there. They'll come up with something."

"We don't have oddities like this around here every day, Mr. Hammer."

"It's Mike. No, I suppose you don't. Which makes this a big story."

She shook her head and her slightly shellacked hair bounced a tad. "Last story anything like this was over a year ago. I doubt it got covered in the big city. We had a spate of grave robberies. Over a period of three years, maybe . . . two, three a year. Then they stopped."

"Random stuff? The graves, I mean. Just any old grave?"

"New ones. Always the graves of women. Attractive women who'd died young, mostly in their twenties, none older than forty. I understand that . . . that *thing* over there is something quite apart, but it's still an odd, grisly, horror-show kind of sight."

"That wasn't a woman," I said, with a nod toward the terrible corpse.

"You're sure?"

"Well, that's a man's hand."

"I . . . I didn't take as close a look as I probably should have. Mr. Hammer . . . Mike . . . when the police lab reports come in, and we know more, I may want to consult with you."

I got a card out and handed it to her. It had office and cell numbers on it. She tucked it in her purse, gave me hers with similar info. Then in a friendly but businesslike way, she gave me her hand and I took it.

It was a lot more attractive than the dead guy's.

Velda, standing in the middle of the reception area of our two-room office, used a remote to turn up the sound on the over-sized wall screen. She was my secretary, partner and fiancee all wrapped up in one beautiful raven-haired bundle. She looked like every older dame wished she did, and even past fifty she could make a white blouse and black skirt seem like something out of Victoria's Secret.

She listened to me being interviewed, commented that I'd been right—they pixelated that mess of a corpse before coming back to the jumpsuited gorgeous gal who wore a properly somber frown.

Melodie Anderson was standing near the gruesome discovery, and Velda and I both caught the moment the news-woman took, during her wrap-up, where she half-turned so nobody would see her swallow deeply to keep from throwing up herself.

Velda said, "Sensitive, isn't she?"

"They don't get much of that upstate," I said.

"Where *do* they exactly? Let's take a look at those shots you got."

She walked to her desk where she could click through the images on her computer screen. I had taken one close-up of the hand and she was focusing on that.

I said, "Pat expects an ID tonight. *If* the prints are registered."

"You ever see a corpse in that condition?" she asked me.

I leaned in to look over her shoulder at the screen. "I've been at a couple of plane crash sites. Saw my share of bodies all mashed together. Looked something like this, yeah. But then, at least, the pieces were fairly recognizable. This kill mixes chunks with coarse hamburger."

"Except for the hand," Velda said softly.

"Except for where it was cut off from the wrist. That was nice and neat."

"How neat?"

"Like they used to say about Jack the Ripper—almost surgical."

The lovely dark eyes narrowed. "Are you sure that tendon was attached to the rest of the . . . pile?"

I shook my head. "We didn't disturb anything. Pat had to get back, so we gave the cops all that we could and left."

"And Pat will give them a full report, I suppose."

"You know Pat, kitten."

Velda backed away from the monitor, turned toward me as I leaned in. She ran her fingers down my cheek. "And I know *you*, lover."

"Think so?"

"Absolutely."

"Spell it out."

"This is one you haven't had before. It's squeezing you already, isn't it? Mike Hammer can't drop this like he should, and let the official world of policedom do its job, can he?"

"Hey, I found the body, doll."

"If you call that a body."

"You want me to forget about it?" I asked her.

Velda gave me that sly look I knew all too well. Her full-lipped mouth was wet and smiled up at me until I saw the edges of her teeth and the sudden flick of her tongue between them.

"Never gave that a thought, big guy," she said. "You can go play with that gory mess all you want. Get your name in the papers some more, like old times. I bet that brunette on the news already has a big crush on you. Daddy issues, maybe."

"Aw, Velda, cut me a break . . ."

She tapped my nose with the tip of her forefinger. "Just let her know that I'm one of your retirement benefits."

My hands went around her waist and as I started to draw her near me, the phone rang.

Pat said, "Mike . . . glad I caught you. Listen, those locals sent that mess *our* way, for processing. The lab has already come up with some interesting stuff."

"What have you got, buddy?"

"Still waiting on a report. Look, have you eaten?"

"No. Why, shall we grab some steak tartar?"

"Very funny. Why don't you and Velda meet me at the French House in a couple of hours."

It must not have been a question because Pat hung up.

I filled Velda in about our new plans for the evening, and we both decided we'd take time to freshen up before going out, and were halfway out of the office when the phone rang again.

"Let the machine get it," I said, and I was just shutting the door when I recognized the voice coming in.

"Mr. Hammer, it's Melodie Anderson, Eye Witness News. Please call me at—"

"Ms. Anderson," I said, grabbing the phone off Velda's desk. "I'm here."

Velda came strolling back in, then deposited herself a few feet from me in a Valkyrie-like stance with her arms folded and her smirk knowing.

"Daddy," she murmured.

"Mr. Hammer," the reporter said, "I was hoping to talk to you tonight. I think I may be on to something. Jason, that's my cameraman, and I are still out chasing down some leads. But I could use your help."

"You want me to come to you?"

"No, I can come into the city. We just have one more stop before calling it a night."

So I invited her to join us at the French House, giving her the address, and she said she might be a little late, but to wait for her.

I hung up and grinned at Velda. "She's joining us tonight. You can warn her off in person."

An eyebrow arched. "Yeah? Well, if you go playing daddy with that babe, buster, Mommy's gonna spank."

"Promises promises," I said, and we headed to her apartment to freshen up. I keep some clothes there. I said it was a long engagement.

The French House had nothing to do with French cuisine. This was an out-of-the way place, strictly deli fare, in a rough patch not far from the Times Square theater district. Velda and I were already on one side of the booth when Pat showed up, a few minutes later, and slid in opposite.

"That hand with the remains," he said. "It didn't belong there."

Velda said, "Well, hello to you, too, Pat. I'm fine thanks."

"Hi Velda," he said, and smiled awkwardly. He still had a thing for her. Then he looked at me and there wasn't any awkwardness in it at all. "Prints came in with an ID. It's a missing person. A famous one."

"Yeah?" I said, chewing a corner of my corned beef-and-Swiss sandwich. "As famous as us, buddy?"

"At least. Victor King, the Broadway producer."

Velda had no smart remarks to make now. She put her cheeseburger down and leaned forward. "What's it been, a month? He went off for a meeting somewhere and never got there."

"*And* never came back," Pat said. "Know where that meeting was?"

"Upstate New York," I said, through another bite.

"You don't impress easily. How about this? That hand was starting to decompose."

"Didn't look like it," I said, chewing.

"The lab boys actually have some microscopes that can see things your ancient eyes can't."

"These ancient eyes are twenty twenty, Pat. Spill it. The big surprise."

He seemed disappointed I sensed that something else was coming. But I knew him like he knew me.

"That hand," he said, "didn't belong to that pile of fresh ground chuck . . . sorry, Velda."

She put down her cheeseburger again.

"They can tell this," I said, using a napkin, "because the pile wasn't decomposing. It was fresh."

"That's part of it," Pat admitted. "But things have come a long way in the detection game since Sherlock Holmes used his first magnifying glass and you throttled your first suspect."

"Yeah?"

"That pile of . . . stuff. That *wasn't* Victor King."

"Blood type didn't match?"

"I'll spare you the gory details, but let's leave it at this: the hand belonged to a man. Everything else was female."

That had been Pat's last big surprise, but the evening held one more: Melodie Anderson didn't show. We waited till near eleven, with me on the cell phone trying the various numbers on the card she'd given me. Nothing. I finally tried her station and got through to the news desk, and she was out. I asked for her home number and was refused.

"Listen," I said to the young-sounding guy, "I got a bad feeling about this. Call her at home, check that she's okay, and tell her Mike Hammer's trying to get in touch with her."

"Okay, dude! Okay."

Dude.

But he did call back, sounding mildly worried himself.

"No answer," he said. "I left a message. Sorry. I'll leave a note for her to call you when she comes in tomorrow."

I thanked him.

We were still in the booth, working on a third round of beers.

"Don't worry about the girl," Pat said. "She probably had a big story come in and got caught up in it. You'll hear from her."

I didn't remind him that the small upstate burg where she lived and worked was damn short on big stories. A pile of human flesh on the roadside was about as big as it got.

That, and grave-robbing.

"Listen," Pat said, pushing aside a mostly finished beer, "there's an aspect of this I haven't gone into. I hesitate to, because I shouldn't be encouraging you."

"King's wife is a suspect," I said.

"Damn you, anyway! How do you know that?"

"Because the letch got married for the fourth time last year. He was fifty-nine and the blushing bride, what? Twenty-five? She probably signed a prenup, and the only way she inherits is if her husband kicks it."

Pat's eyes were half-lidded. "Which makes her a suspect."

"Not if he just disappears. Unless she doesn't mind a seven-year wait before King is declared legally dead."

"Only now he *is* dead. Now that that hand has turned up."

"That doesn't make him dead."

Pat eyes weren't half-lidded anymore. "That's right. That pile of flesh *wasn't* him. So what are you going to do, Mike? Wade into this?"

I handed him the check. "What do you think I'm gonna do? Play the hand I got dealt."

The next morning, around ten, I was sitting in the lavish living room of Victor King's penthouse apartment on upper Fifth Avenue, with a view on Central Park. The furnishings were vintage art deco and what wasn't white was black, and what wasn't blond wood was chrome, and everything had curves. Including Mrs. King, who was also blonde.

As expected, she was a very lovely twenty-five or so, the stark red of her lounging pajamas matching her finger- and toenails, jumping out at me like the devil against the white of the couch, her legs crossed, a hand caressing a knee. Her mouth was similarly red, but her eyes were baby blue with blue eye shadow and a sleepy look, like a cheerleader on her third beer after the big game.

I couldn't imagine any man wanting to sleep with her, unless he was heterosexual and had a pulse.

The funny thing was, she was wearing the same sexy red p.j.'s in an oversize elaborately framed photographic portrait of her husband and herself over a white marble fireplace. Victor King was in some kind of yachting outfit and had Ricardo Montalbán hair and the kind of tan the sun has nothing to do with. In the picture she was seated, with her chin up and smiling a little, knowing what she had, and he was standing next to her, with an arm around the top of the chair, not his wife, like he knew what he had, too.

But the picture couldn't capture her best feature—luminous, creamy skin that damn near glowed. I supposed someday nature or old age would catch up to her and draw some lines in. Right now it was smooth. So very smooth, drawn tight over apple cheeks in a way plastic surgeons could only envy.

She must have caught me looking from her to the portrait behind her, and she grinned. Suddenly she looked like the kid she must have been before she realized she could parlay her looks into money, if not on the stage then from some sugar daddy.

"Victor has three more of those," she said, and her voice was breathy and childish, although unlike the outfit it was no act, "in storage somewhere. Wives numbers one, two and three."

"Were they wearing red jammies, too?"

That stopped her for a second and then she laughed. She snorted when she laughed, which made her suddenly human.

"I guess I was trying to make a point," she said, and gestured to herself, her breasts making two points actually, under the satin. "Victor was happy with me, Mr. Hammer. He wasn't running around on me. Would you?"

"No," I admitted, "but I don't put on Broadway musicals with tons of cute kiddos in the chorus. That's where he found you, right? And numbers one through three?"

"Number one was his high school sweetheart, actually," she said. "I'm going to smoke. Would you like to? I picture you smoking."

"Go ahead. But none for me, thanks. I gave up cigarettes a long, long time ago. Probably why I'm still on this side of the grass."

I bet myself she would use a cigarette holder and won. It made her look even more like a kid playing dress-up.

I waited for her to blow a smoke ring, then said, "I appreciate the phone call, Mrs. King, and the offer of employment. But I already have a case."

"Isn't it the *same* case? The papers were having a lot of fun this morning with you discovering Victor's body."

Had Pat or anyone official told her yet that the hand was her husband's, but that grisly ball of kibbles and bits wasn't?

Should I?

"Mr. Hammer, there's been a lot of speculation that Victor was running around on me. I assure you he wasn't."

"You seem confident."

"Victor was not a young man. I serviced him at least once a day."

"Service with a smile?"

"Service with variety and imagination and if he had the energy and ability to seek more fun elsewhere, more power to him."

My chair probably won a prize at the New York World's Fair in '39, but I shifted in it, looking for a comfortable position, and wasn't that good a detective.

"Mrs. King, why would you tolerate your husband running around on you? Assuming he *did* find the energy and ability."

Her smile wouldn't have been one were it any smaller. "Mr. Hammer, I am an adequate dancer in a town full of great ones, and my singing is only so so. As an actress, I'm pretty good, but no Streep. I could eke out an existence on Broadway in bit parts and chorus line gigs, for a while, but then it would be back to Minot, North Dakota, for me. And you know what, Mr. Hammer? Minot, North Dakota, is goddamn cold."

"I bet it is."

"I like my life with Victor. I wish I could have him back."

Maybe, but not to where there were any tears in those baby blues or any quaver in that breathy baby voice.

"But if he's dead," she said, matter of fact, "I inherit everything. He, uh, never had any children . . ."

Except the ones he married.

". . . and no close relatives. So it would be all mine."

"Which is a hell of a murder motive."

She nodded, struck a regal pose worthy of Jean Harlow. I wondered if she knew who Jean Harlow was.

"But I didn't kill him," she said, "or have him killed, either.

SHIN

The police have been hounding me for this whole month that Victor's been missing, and the papers just *love* the story."

"I don't remember them making a suspect out of you."

"No, but they will, now that his body has turned up."

What the hell. She had a right to know.

"Don't tell the cops I told you," I said, sitting forward, "but that body wasn't your husband."

Her eyes popped. "What?"

"The hand belonged to him," I said, and filled her in.

She put the cigarette-in-holder in a tray and got up and began to pace. Then she planted herself before me and asked, "Could he still be alive?"

"Do you want him to be?"

Her eyes and nostrils flared. "Yes! I love him. You don't have to believe me, but a young woman *can* love an older man. It *is* possible."

What was it Velda said? Daddy issues.

"You wanted to hire me for something," I said, gesturing for her to sit back down.

She did, both legs on the floor now, sitting on the edge of a couch cushion with hands clasped in her lap. "I wanted you to look into his murder. I wanted you to clear me. But what does this *mean*, his hand being found next to that . . . that thing?"

"I don't know. I'll be honest with you, kid. I was going to look into it for nothing."

"Why?"

"Because it's not good for business for Mike Hammer to find corpses on the roadside and just go on about his merry way. Certain things are expected of me."

She smiled a little. "Like certain things are expected of a woman who looks like me?"

"Time was," I said with a wistful sigh, "somebody who looks like you was a 'girl.' Now it's politically incorrect. Now you're a woman. And you'll need to be."

"Why?"

I stood. "Because I don't figure there's any way this can turn out in a good way for you. Or your husband. Especially your husband."

She rose. "If Victor is dead, and you clear me, that would be a good thing. A good thing worth ten thousand dollars from me to you."

Thirty years ago, hell, twenty years ago, I might have negotiated for a different kind of payment. And even now thoughts stirred—she liked older men, she knew how to keep them satisfied. In my mind, all that red satin was a puddle and all that luminous skin was in my arms, in my hands. . . .

"Ten grand will be fine," I said. "It'll go a long way toward my retirement."

I sat across from Sergeant Mal Tooney in a booth in a diner about five miles from where I'd found Victor King's hand next to that ghastly pile.

"I'm glad to meet with you, Mr. Hammer," he said. "Because I *am* concerned."

The heavyset cop had a cup of black coffee in front of him, but hadn't touched it. He was in uniform, his cap off, exposing his dying hair. By way of contrast, his eyebrows were wild, shaggy patches.

I had called Tooney from the office this morning, before taking the meeting with Mrs. King, to ask him to check up on the absent Melodie Anderson. I'd already tried the TV station and she hadn't shown up for work. Neither had her cameraman. Calls from the station manager to both had come up bupkus. I asked Tooney to look into it.

That was this morning in New York. This was that afternoon, upstate.

"I checked both the Anderson woman's house and this Jason kid's apartment," he said. "Talked to neighbors, got the super to let me in the kid's place. No sign of either of them."

"They were in a TV station van."

"Yes, and it's still signed out to them. Both their cars are in the station's parking lot. Listen, this could be bad."

"Yeah. Can you rally the troops?"

"Not for twenty-four hours I can't. They aren't missing persons yet. But considering what we . . . what *you* . . . found yesterday? I just have a bad, sick feeling."

A waitress came over and refilled my coffee, which made Tooney remember his. He sipped it.

"Sarge," I said, "I know for a fact Melodie Anderson was running down leads on this thing. She told me so. I think she may have been on to something—she didn't show for a meeting with me last night."

"She really could be in trouble."

"She could be dead," I said. I stirred sweetener and Half-and-Half in. "She mentioned something about grave robberies in this neck of the woods."

He frowned and the shaggy eyebrows met, making one big caterpillar. "That goes back a while. There was a string of 'em, but the latest was over a year ago. Why, you think what you found was a dug-up corpse?"

"No. That was fresh meat."

An old gal in the booth behind Tooney turned and gave me a dirty look.

"And the lab reports," I went on, giving her a wink, "didn't mention anything like embalming procedures having been done. But the Anderson girl had a hunch there was a connection, so any leads she was chasing down could have had something to do with that."

"Well, it was young women's corpses," he said, "exclusively. I just figured it was some nut who liked to have sex with dead bodies. What do they call those guys?"

The gal and her companion, another biddy, huffed and got up and left. They may have been disgusted with us, but they sure finished their food first.

"Necrophiliacs," I said.

Tooney's shaggy eyebrows were in two pieces again and climbing up his forehead. "You know, we had this report . . . screwy report . . . from some kids a while back. Maybe . . . three months ago?"

"Yeah?"

"Well, I never took it too seriously. They were just high school kids who were hanging out at a local cemetery at midnight, drinking and fooling around. That's a place where kids do that, sometimes, just a quiet place where they can party."

"Who's to complain?"

"Right. Only, the cemetery *did* complain, and I went over there in a squad and we rounded up half a dozen kids, and they were pretty high."

"Liquor or dope?"

"Some of both. Anyway, there were enough of 'em that we had to call for a van. And while we were waiting, they started in on, 'What are you giving *us* a bad time for? Why don't you round up that Looney Tunes?' I said, 'What Looney Tunes?'

And these kids claimed that they sneaked up on this guy who was dancing around naked in the moonlight."

"Okay. You have my interest, Sarge."

"The guy was dancing to some kind of classical music on an old cassette player, and just doing some wild, crazy dance in and around the tombstones. Throwing his arms up and around. Reckless abandon, like."

"Naked."

"Well, that's what they said, at first. But two of the kids said he wasn't naked. That he was naked under some kind of . . . skin."

"Skin?"

"Like he skinned somebody and stitched it up into some kind of crazy, awful outfit."

"A human skin."

"That's what two of the kids said, Mr. Hammer. And not just a human skin."

"Huh?"

"A woman's skin."

And now the people in the booth behind me left, too.

What sort of leads would Melodie Anderson and her camera-man be following up?

That cemetery maybe? But the manager of the Life Transition Center at Greenwood Memorial said Melodie Anderson hadn't come around yesterday afternoon.

"Or if she did," he said, in the mellow baritone of a preacher, which probably came in handy dealing with the bereaved, "we failed to make contact. An internment had my full attention into the early evening."

I was sitting across from the shrunken little guy in a small modern office off a much larger showroom of cremation urns and coffins, bronze markers, and granite memorials. It was like a ghoulish gift shop here at the Life Transition Center. I'd helped my share of miscreants make their life transitions, but I didn't feel at home.

The manager's desk was neat and so was he, no mortician black for this character, just earth tones, like the copper sweater and tan shirt with burnt-orange tie. His eyes were sleepy and brown in a face shaped like an acorn squash.

I asked, "Have there been any other reports of this crazy guy dancing around in the moonlight?"

He pursed his lips in a skeptical smile. "Mr. Hammer, a man of your experience should hardly take seriously some wild tale concocted by drunken little twerps."

And then he was off on a bitch fest about how much trouble these local kids caused, partying on his grounds.

"Your night watchman," I said, "hasn't reported anything similar to what those kids said?"

"Mr. Hammer, we don't have a night watchman. A security company makes regular rounds after hours. We're just another business on their schedule."

"A patrol vehicle?"

"That is correct."

"Regular rounds?"

"I believe so."

"So somebody could time those trips and take advantage to disturb one of your graves, or put on a bare-ass dance recital."

He shrugged his lack of concern. "The last grave disturbance was over a year ago." Then the sleepy eyes woke up. "But those damn *kids* are drinking and getting high and fornicating, every time I turn around!"

I tried to remember the last time I heard "fornicating" used in conversation, and couldn't.

"Maybe they've learned to time those trips, too," I suggested.

He had no opinion.

I thanked him and soon had made a transition out into a fall afternoon turned crisp and cold. Perfect weather for football.

Or Halloween.

I was in my car, pulled off the side of the road about where I had yesterday. No Pat Chambers to discuss things with this time. Just me and some thoughts, tumblers turning but refusing to unlock their secret. What kind of leads had that lovely reporter tracked, if she hadn't tried the cemetery?

Somebody had carried, not dragged, that mangled body through the nearby woods. Who might have seen that? A hunter? Maybe a farmer, on a nearby spread? Melodie might have tooled that TV station van around to the nearest side road and stopped to knock on farmhouse doors. This was harvest time, though, and she might find nobody home.

Or maybe she did find somebody home.

I had another two hours of daylight, but I got the pocket flash from the glove compartment and dropped it in my suit-coat pocket, just in case. I was going exploring and how long I'd be and where I'd wind up, who could say?

And like any good jungle explorer, I had an elephant gun along—the Colt .45 automatic variety, designed for military use a long time ago.

Starting where the chewed-up body had been dumped, I found a nearby spot in the bushes that provided something of a path. If those sorry remains had been in plastic or otherwise wrapped, there would be no blood trail to follow. But the brush was thick enough that you could see where someone had moved through, snapping twigs underfoot and branches on either side. Only a few minutes later, I was in the trees, where crushed leaves on the forest floor marked recent passage.

Had a madman walked naked through these trees with a package of human meat wrapped up in a tidy bundle? Or had he been clothed—perhaps in the skin of the very victim whose mangled remains he meant to discard?

But he was doing more than just discarding those remains. That was the one thing I *had* figured out. That hand, from a previous victim, was left with what had been a living, breathing woman by a killer sophisticated enough to know that the papers were full of efforts to find that previous victim. But that killer was *not* sophisticated enough to realize things like DNA tests and other laboratory forensics could determine that the hand and the corpse did not go together.

That made an awful, terrible sense, but it did not explain where the rest of victim number one had gone to—the man who belonged to that hand.

My client's husband—Victor King.

It was about ten minutes from the roadside to the end of the trees. Now I found myself at the edge of a harvested corn field, like a scarecrow who had wandered off his beat. To the right, I could make out the tops of a farmhouse, a silo, a barn. Walking along between where the line of trees stopped and the field began, I made my way there.

The farmhouse was probably one hundred years old but wore a facelift of siding that dated back maybe twenty. The English-style gabled barn was gray weathered wood but sturdy-looking. The silo was by far the newest of the structures. No sign of farm animals, though I spotted a new-looking tractor and a sizeable thresher and other well-maintained equipment near the harvested field that stretched everywhere. No cars were visible on the gravel apron around the house nor was there any sign of activity. A driveway angled through the trees to a gravel road that would give access to the highway.

This appeared to be a normal, small, prosperous working farm.

I figured maybe I would just go knock on the door, but that was when I noticed something in the thicket just off the gravel apron—something metallic that glinted off the dying sun. I went over and had a look, peeling back leafy branches, some thorny, to do so.

The TV station van was tucked back there. Not parked—hidden away. All its doors were locked. I looked in the windows to see if I could spot any blood or sign of struggle, or even a body.

Nothing.

Through the van's rear windows I could make out valuable video production equipment. Somehow I didn't think Melodie Anderson and her camera guy Jason were in that house doing an interview about the struggle of the small family farmer in the face of corporate farming.

Dusk had turned the landscape a cool blue, lending it an unreality, and the idyllic nature of the farm seemed worthy of a sentimental print you might buy in a mall frame shop. Yet I could feel something wrong, a feeling admittedly fueled by the discovery of that van, but also a prickling of the hairs on the back of my neck that came from years of dealing with dangerous situations.

With no sign of a vehicle, nobody seemed to be home. My

suitcoat hanging open for easy access to the .45, I decided to find out. I knocked on the front door and rang the bell. Nothing.

I did the same in back. Again, nothing.

Over at the barn, the big doors were padlocked shut; looking in the windows did no good—they were wire-and-glass jobs that didn't reveal anything in the dark space.

Returning to the house, I tried the back and it was locked. But I could see the door wasn't completely closed—the wood was warped enough to make it stick, and the lock hadn't caught. A shoulder easily pushed my way in, no harm done.

The kitchen was clean, probably remodeled in the '70s. The refrigerator was empty but for milk and beer and some cold cuts. The wastebasket revealed fast-food sacks and Chinese restaurant cartons. Somebody here existed on carry out, only this kitchen had none of the slovenly aftermath that often accompanied that lifestyle.

As I prowled the place with my .45 in hand, slow, careful, listening for any sound that wasn't made by me, I found rooms that were so clean, nobody seemed to live here. The TV in the living room was circa the '70s or '80s, and none of the furniture looked any newer, though a baby grand seemed much older. A fireplace had a bearskin rug in front of it, and on the mantle were framed photographs of a jug-eared buck-toothed boy posing alternately with his mother and father.

Mom would pose with the boy, seated next to him or standing nearby, with the funny-looking kid playing various musical instruments—a violin, a flute, and that baby grand. Mom had given him the big cow eyes, but she was otherwise very attractive—handsome, like they used to say.

The pictures with his father, who had bequeathed the kid

those jug ears, were all posed outside in hunting jackets and full gear, often holding up dead ducks and geese and pheasants by the webbed feet, sometimes bending over dead deer and even the late bear I was standing on now.

Over the mantle was a huge photograph of the family that immediately reminded me of the one of Victor King and his current trophy wife—Mother was seated and Dad had an arm around the upper chair, with a smile of ownership. Two things made the photo creepy—first, it was not a color shot, rather one of those pastel hand-colored jobs; and second, the boy at about age seven was sitting on his mama's lap.

Somebody had a seriously screwed-up upbringing.

If Melodie and her camera guy were being held hostage here, the basement seemed a good place to check. But it turned out to be one big space, empty of anything but a washer and drier setup that was the only item in this house that didn't seem to date back a couple decades.

Upstairs I found bedrooms, and from the look of the rooms, one was Daddy's, one was Mommy's, and another Baby Boy's. Daddy's was as much a den as a bedroom with a heavily antlered deer's head and some mounted fish and various hunting prints. Several bookcases, too, running to Zane Grey and Louis L'Amour. Mommy had a very feminine room, all blues and pinks and frills, including floral wallpaper and a four-poster bed. In her closet were clothes dating to the '80s.

Neither room smelled musty. The clothing had a freshly laundered scent. No moth balls at work up here. Somebody was maintaining these two shrines.

What about Baby Boy's room?

Well, it was as messy as the rest of the house was neat. A clutter of magazines, books, VHS tapes, DVDs and video games covered the floor. A small but new-looking TV was on a stand with electronic gear below—*not* '70s and '80s vintage. Time had moved on in this space, but in a messy way. This was a hoarder's hideaway with pictures of naked women from men's magazines Scotch-taped to wallpapered walls. He'd have to crawl over junk to get to the single, small unmade bed, which was red and black and in the shape of a racing car. A laptop computer shared his night stand with magazines (*Popular Mechanics*, *Hustler*), several soda cans, and a box of Kleenex.

I poked in the dresser and saw neatness again, stacked and freshly laundered work shirts and jeans, including overalls. Jockey shorts and t-shirts were outnumbered by pairs of long-johns. Then I looked in the closet.

Hanging there, like crucified martyrs, were the dried, neatly stitched together skins of at least a dozen humans.

The women outnumbered the men by half. Hangers slipped under the loose shoulders held them in neat array, eyeless masklike faces hanging backward like hoods. Even the feet were still attached, like grotesque Dr. Denton's.

Only the hands were gone.

I stepped back. My tongue was thick in my mouth. My heart was starting to pound, and a burger I'd wolfed at that diner was trying to make a break for it. I have seen a lot of things in my long and storied career, but I had never seen the like of this, and I am here to tell you that Mrs. Hammer's little boy Michael was scared shitless.

I got the hell out of there.

Out of the room, out of the house, moving in a tight circle as I went, ready for him from wherever he might spring, some grotesque middle-aged version of that jug-eared, cow-eyed boy. I had my .45 in hand and if the man of the castle, or whatever the hell he was, came at me, I was ready to blast him to Kingdom Come.

But he didn't, and I was outside, gulping in cool air, and darkness had fallen. Hadn't it, though.

Still no sign of a vehicle. Gripping the .45, I returned to the barn. If Melodie and Jason were being held anywhere on this property, that seemed the most likely place. I didn't want to deal with that padlock on the barn's big front doors—if the owner showed up, he could spot that too easily. But there was a smaller set of double doors in back, also with a padlock, and the butt of the .45 knocked that off, hasp and all.

I went in. Hay lofts loomed on either side, and a row of empty animal stalls were along the left, with various farm implements, big and small, arranged under the loft overhang at right, on work benches, on pegboard. The floor was poured cement, much newer than the weathered gray outer structure. The cement sloped to several drains. Some pools of oil indicated vehicles might on occasion get stored here, but the most striking sight was the small thresher machine—if that's what it was—that sat in the middle of the space. About the size of a Volkswagen Beetle, it was a patched-together thing, some of it bare metal, some parts bright red, others green, salvaged or scavenged from other farm equipment.

Oddly, it immediately recalled that pile of mismatched and chewed-up human parts that had started me on this search— it was pieces of this machine and that one welded together. To this city boy, it seemed a thresher, but the top section was flat with conveyor rollers and seemed to feed a boxy metallic maw, while on the other side of the thing, below, was another squared-off spout where whatever you fed in came out. A big black metal tray was under there . . . and I knew.

It was a skinning machine.

You laid your victim on top, mercifully dead (one would hope), and that seemed likely because there were no straps. The body would pass on the mini-conveyer through the metallic innards whose blades separated flesh from muscle and bone and organ. The design was as clever as it was fiendish, because the blades wouldn't cut and churn until well within the metal maw, making blood spatter little or nil. I could even see the handles where you lifted the upper part, like a photocopier, to remove the "garment" just created. The residue, in no particular shape or form, would plop into the tray for disposal.

Normally the warped genius who had devised this beauty might have gotten rid of that refuse in any number of ways. Maybe there were pigs somewhere around here he could feed it to. Maybe this human mulch enriched his soil, who knew?

But I'd been right—he'd moved from grave-robbing to way-laying motorists, only he'd made a bad choice stopping Victor King. My hunch was King indeed had been stepping out on his beautiful young wife, because I didn't figure the inventor of this machine would have stopped him if a lovely young woman hadn't been along for the ride.

Then, in recent days, it became necessary for Baby Boy to leave Victor King's hand next to the latest chewed-up corpse, to stop the hunt for the producer.

Only the hands were gone.

He cut off the hands and saved them. Why? Perhaps the hands didn't make a good trip through his gizmo. Too many fingers and working parts. Or maybe he just liked to have full range of expression for his artistic fingers when he was doing his dance. Maybe he was even smart enough to save the hands for the very purpose he'd put King's to—allowing a victim to turn up dead, if a disappearance was making too much heat.

I called Pat on the cell. Quickly I told him where I was, that I'd wandered into a psycho's playground, and said to inform the locals and get out here himself.

"Any sign of the newscaster?" he asked.

"No," I said, and then I heard it.

The muffled sound of someone trying to talk through a restraint.

"Just get out here," I said, and clicked off.

I'd been so transfixed by the skinner that I hadn't searched the place, and in the two stalls nearest those front double doors, I found them—the kid Jason, naked, his mouth duct-taped, his hands duct-taped behind him, his ankles, too. Unconscious.

Melodie was awake in her stall, her eyes huge and luminous in the glowing face, streaked with dirt and tears. She'd been given the duct-tape treatment, too, and like her cameraman, lay sprawled on the cement floor, which was dusted with hay. She, too, was naked, her skin pale and lovely despite the obscene display.

Bending over her, I removed the tape and soon she was in my arms, hysterical, crying, gasping, half-screaming, "Mr. Hammer! Mr. Hammer! Thank God."

"Easy, baby. Is that kid okay?"

"That crazy farmer gave Jason some kind of drug—something in a big hypo, like you'd give a horse. I don't know if he's alive or not."

I checked in the stall next door. The kid had a pulse. On the slow side maybe, but a pulse.

She was at my side, naked and shivering but also demanding. "Get me out of here! You have *got* to get us *out* of here."

I slipped an arm around her, her flesh cool and smooth to the touch. "The cops are on the way."

"Can't you drive us?"

"My car's too far. We're better off waiting."

Her eyes and nostrils flared. "You can't be *serious!*"

"Your van's out there, but God knows where the keys are. I'd have to carry that cameraman of yours like a baby, and if our host drove up while we were trying to get to the highway, or to my car . . . no. You just go back in your stall."

"*What?*"

"Go back in your stall, and put that duct tape loosely over your mouth. Play possum."

"I will not!"

My hand gripped her shoulder tight. "You will. Put your hands behind your back and pretend nothing's changed since you last saw him. With luck, the cops'll be here before he shows. If not, I don't want him coming in and thinking anything's wrong."

She got it. "Before you jump him, you mean."

"Something like that."

Reluctantly, she did as I told her. When she was properly in place, I leaned down and gave her a kiss on the forehead, told her everything would be all right. Like Daddy.

Then I went to the stall adjacent to Jason, where I figured to position myself, and had yet another shock.

A pile of hands in a big stainless steel tray were in there. Like they were ready to be put out on a salad bar. Some were shrunken and mummified. Others looked fresher.

I took the next stall down.

And waited. Waited for the cop sirens. Waited as what was left of dusk darkened to night through those wire-and-glass windows.

SHIN

When he came in, he was wearing somebody.

Some beautiful woman, most likely, but Melodie's crazy farmer wasn't beautiful. He was hideous. He was inside the skin, with its long flowing hair and empty drooping breast sacks, his hands popping out of the sleeves of dried stitched flesh, and the cow eyes were huge and wild in the empty facial sockets.

What happened to that little boy who grew up in that house? What were his *daddy issues? What were his* mommy *issues?*

Something to do with killing and skinning and stuffing dead creatures, something else to do with artistic leanings and maybe the wrong feelings toward a mommy who had him sit on her lap.

Somebody, other than God, had made this monster.

But I would leave it to my betters to feel sorry for him. Me, I had no intention of letting him plead insanity and wind up in a minimum security hospital where they could untangle his wires and release him, or maybe before that, he'd just go over the fence some night.

Unless those cops showed very damn soon, I was going to kill the bastard. And I was just moving out of the stall when he rushed over to a bench where he touched a finger to a button on a vintage cassette player and a very distorted, scratchy version of "Hall of the Mountain King" began to play.

Behind him the double doors were open and moonlight crept in and smothered him in ivory, and he began to dance. Dancing in someone else's skin. Dancing in the moonlight.

And you know what? He wasn't half bad.

I stepped out and showed him the .45.

He froze in mid-balletic stance. "Who . . . who are you?"

I didn't have a chance to say anything, because Melodie

made a break for it. She had seen those open doors and he was positioned in front of her, where she didn't think he could see her, and she just went for it.

But he *did* see her, and grabbed her from behind, flung her around by the wrist, making a human shield of her, all that glowing living flesh blocking that creped, stitched Frankenstein suit with a madman in it. And as I closed in, he moved defiantly my way and kicked out with a foot and turned on that thresher and it chugged and grunted and groaned and whined.

Was it hungry?

"I'll stick her in it!" he yelled.

He had to yell, because his contraption was loud, blotting out the cassette player, and it seemed to shake the old barn's walls, and to its churning rhythm, we moved in our own dance until he was over under the loft overhang and snatched a sharp sickle off the wall. Then its blade was at her throat like he was the grim reaper and I was just some damn human being who couldn't do a goddamn thing about it.

And I couldn't.

Not unless I could get a clear shot at his head, shutting off his motor reflexes. Then Melodie would be fine, and he'd fall to the cement as limp as his skin suit. But he was on the small side, and she was a tall drink of water, and I could not find a decent damn trajectory.

Meanwhile, that goddamn machine chugged and grunted and whined, wanting to be useful, wanting to be fed.

I raised my left hand in surrender, knelt and set the .45 on the cement. Then I stood and raised the other hand. He peeked up over her shoulder and smiled. Putting my gun down and my hands up had been enough to satisfy him.

He shoved her to one side and ran through the double doors. I had the .45 in hand in seconds and put one in his ass that sent him sprawling to the gravel. The .45's roar was a percussive grace note in the terrible chugging song of the skinning machine. I ran out there, throwing a long shadow in the moonlight and pulled back the human hood to expose his jug-eared head and grabbed a handful of thick, greasy hair and dragged him back into the barn.

Melodie had Jason on his feet. The naked kid was coming around, and she had removed the duct tape from his mouth, wrists and ankles.

"Go wait over by the house," I said, working it up over the industrial chug of the machine. "I'll be there in a while."

She nodded and drunk-walked him away.

But as she went, she looked over her shoulder at me. Very small, her voice called out: "My father always liked you! How you *did* things!"

Sirens finally. Distant. Probably just enough time.

Because I knew what the girl meant.

I dragged him by the hair and he made a snail trail of red on the cement. Then I stripped the human garment off him and rested it as respectfully as I could a distance away. He was crawling toward the double doors, and was almost there when I stepped in front of him and shut us in, the only light provided by the moon coming in those wired windows.

He was screaming and kicking, a big hairless baby but for his head of hair and pubic curls, and he howled when I slammed him on his back on top of his invention, hard enough to daze him, his feet at the maw. The machine was still chugging, the conveyor belt going, blades whirring, and he was immediately traveling into his own dark imagination. His screams lasted until he was in up to his knees, and I'd been right, there was no blood blowback at all, just a spattery sound you could barely make out over the mechanical music.

He was just about to pass out when I got it in.

I grinned at him.

"More than one way to skin a cat," I said.

MICKEY SPILLANE (1918–2006) was an American crime writer. Many of his novels featured the detective Mike Hammer. Born in Brooklyn, New York, Spillane sold his first story to a pulp magazine by the time he graduated from high school. He served as a fighter pilot in the army air corps in World War II, and published his first novel, *I, the Jury*, in 1947. With over two hundred twenty-five million copies of his books sold internationally, Spillane ranks as one of the world's most popular mystery writers.

MAX ALLAN COLLINS is an award-winning writer of mysteries, comics, thrillers, screenplays, and historical fiction. His graphic novel *Road to Perdition* was the basis for the 2002 Academy Award–winning film of the same name. Collins cofounded the International Association of Media Tie-In Writers and studied at the Iowa Writers' Workshop. He collaborated with Mickey Spillane on several projects and is completing a number of the Mike Hammer novels that Spillane left unfinished. Collins lives in Iowa with his wife, author Barbara Collins.

MYSTERIOUSPRESS.COM

Otto Penzler, owner of the Mysterious Bookshop in Manhattan, founded the Mysterious Press in 1975. Penzler quickly became known for his outstanding selection of mystery, crime, and suspense books, both from his imprint and in his store. The imprint was devoted to printing the best books in these genres, using fine paper and top dust-jacket artists, as well as offering many limited, signed editions.

Now the Mysterious Press has gone digital, publishing ebooks through **MysteriousPress.com**.

MysteriousPress.com offers readers essential noir and suspense fiction, hard-boiled crime novels, and the latest thrillers from both debut authors and mystery masters. Discover classics and new voices, all from one legendary source.

FIND OUT MORE AT

WWW.MYSTERIOUSPRESS.COM

FOLLOW US:

@emysteries and Facebook.com/MysteriousPressCom

MysteriousPress.com is one of a select group of publishing partners of Open Road Integrated Media, Inc.

THE MYSTERIOUS BOOKSHOP, founded in 1979, is located in Manhattan's Tribeca neighborhood. It is the oldest and largest mystery-specialty bookstore in America.

The shop stocks the finest selection of new mystery hardcovers, paperbacks, and periodicals. It also features a superb collection of signed modern first editions, rare and collectable works, and Sherlock Holmes titles. The bookshop issues a free monthly newsletter highlighting its book clubs, new releases, events, and recently acquired books.

58 Warren Street
info@mysteriousbookshop.com
(212) 587-1011
Monday through Saturday
11:00 a.m. to 7:00 p.m.

FIND OUT MORE AT:

www.mysteriousbookshop.com

FOLLOW US:

@TheMysterious and Facebook.com/MysteriousBookshop

OPEN ROAD

INTEGRATED MEDIA

Find a full list of our authors and
titles at www.openroadmedia.com

FOLLOW US
@OpenRoadMedia